Miranda

***Also by Linda Lael Miller
in Large Print:***

The Legacy
Daniel's Bride
Forever and the Night

Springwater Seasons
Rachel
Savannah

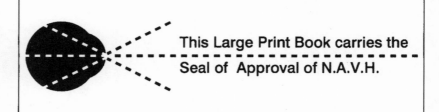

This Large Print Book carries the
Seal of Approval of N.A.V.H.

Linda Lael Miller

SPRINGWATER SEASONS
Book 3

Miranda

Thorndike Press • Thorndike, Maine

1631 3759

Published in 1999 by arrangement with Pocket Books, a division of Simon & Schuster, Inc.

Thorndike Large Print ® Americana Series.

The tree indicium is a trademark of Thorndike Press.

The text of this Large Print edition is unabridged.
Other aspects of the book may vary from the original edition.

Set in 16 pt. Plantin by Juanita Macdonald.

Printed in the United States on permanent paper.

Library of Congress Cataloging-in-Publication Data

Miller, Linda Lael.
  Miranda / Linda Lael Miller.
    p.   cm. — (Springwater seasons ; 3)
  ISBN 0-7862-2159-3 (lg. print : hc : alk. paper)
  1. Large type books.   I. Title.   II. Series: Miller, Linda Lael. Springwater seasons ; 3.
  [PS3563.I41373M57   1999]
  813´.54—dc21   99-36091

For Gina Centrello
Grazie

1

Fall 1875

"I've got two kids to tend to, and hogs to butcher," Landry announced forthrightly, that crisp, early October morning, in the dining room of the Springwater station. "Potatoes and turnips to dig, too, and fields to plow under. The fact is, I need a wife in the worst way." He paused, hat in hand, colored up a little, and cleared his throat. "So I've come to ask if — well, if you'd marry me."

It wasn't the most romantic proposal, Miranda Leebrook reflected, but she'd wanted Landry Kildare for a husband from the moment she clapped eyes on him a couple of months back, while the Hargreaves house was being raised, and she wasn't about to refuse his offer. Besides, she and little Isaiah-or-Ezekiel couldn't expect to stay on with the McCaffreys forever. Heaven knew the baby's real father didn't want either of them, and Pa and his woman,

Lorelei, were long gone.

Landry was a handsome man, with his mischievous hazel eyes and wavy brown hair, and Miranda enjoyed looking at him on any account. Now, gazing into that earnest face, Miranda tried without success to think up a bright and witty remark, something Rachel might say, or Savannah.

Landry glanced around — June-bug and Jacob McCaffrey were pointedly absent — and cleared his throat again. "Of course I won't expect you to — well, what I mean is, you'll have a while to get used to things." A hot rush of crimson washed up his neck to pulse in his lower jaw. "Having a husband and the like." His expression, normally boyish and winsome, proceeded from bleak panic to pure desperation. "What I'm trying to say is, you'll have your own room and all the privacy you want. Until — until you're ready —"

She couldn't resist touching him any longer, and laid the tip of an index finger to his mouth. His lips felt warm and supple, and an odd little jolt of pleasure rocketed through her hand and up her arm to burst, a faint, delicious ache, in a soft fold of her heart. "Jacob and Miss June-bug warrant that you're a good man," she said quietly. "That's all the say-so I need. I'll have you for a husband, Mr. Kildare, if you truly want me for a wife."

He swallowed visibly. "I want you, all right," he said. He averted his gaze, then made himself meet her eyes again. "I guess every woman likes to hear pretty words at a time like this. The plain truth is, I don't have any to say. I loved my wife, Caroline, and I never got over losing her. I don't reckon I'll ever feel just that way about anybody again. But I'll be good to you, Miranda, and I'll raise your little one like he was my own. I'm not a rich man, but I can provide for the both of you, and I'll never bring shame on you, nor lay a hand to either one of you in anger."

She wished he could have claimed to love her, for she surely cherished deep if undefined feelings toward him, but at the same time she knew it was better that he hadn't. He'd have been lying, and she would have known it full well, and never given weight to another word he said from that moment until the day one of them died. Young as she was, barely eighteen, Miranda understood that no alliance could stand, let alone thrive, without trust.

"I guess we should get on with it, then," she said, and blushed herself. She was painfully certain that neither Rachel nor Savannah would ever say anything so stupid when their whole future hung in the balance, and with it, that of their child.

"I'll speak to Jacob," Landry said, with a slight, nervous nod. "About saying the words over us and all, I mean. You might want to get your things ready while I'm about that."

She replied with a nod of her own. She had very few belongings — just four dresses, two made by the industrious June-bug, and two donated by Savannah Parrish, the Doc's wife. There was a stack of flour-sack diapers and some little clothes for the baby, too, and a reading primer Rachel Hargreaves had given her. Rachel was a schoolmarm, despite her marriage and prominent pregnancy, and she'd been helping Miranda with her reading now and again. She could make out the words all right, it wasn't that, but the task was difficult.

Perhaps twenty minutes had passed when Jacob hobbled in, supported by his cane. He was tall, but his big frame had wasted. The light had gone out of his eyes since his heart had nearly given out on him, and he didn't hold forth of a Sunday morning as often as before, but the nearest justice of the peace was in Choteau, and he was the only real preacher for miles around.

June-bug hastily summoned Savannah for a second witness, and when she'd arrived, beaming with delight at the prospect of a wedding so soon after her own, Miranda and Landry took their awkward places before Jacob, both of them listening earnestly to every word he said and responding whenever he asked them to speak.

And so Miranda Leebrook was married, and became Miranda Kildare, all in the course of an October morning. She wore her best dress, a blue calico, and the cornbread June-bug had baked for the midday meal served as wedding cake.

There was no party, no dancing, like when the Doc and Savannah got hitched, but Miranda didn't care about any of that. She and little Isaiah-or-Ezekiel were part of a family now; they had a home to go to, and folks to call their own, and a lifetime of unsullied days, just waiting to dawn.

Her heart sang when Landry helped her into the seat of his well-used buckboard, then stepped aside so June-bug could hand up the baby, solid and heavy in his bundle of blankets. Then Landry was beside her in the wagon, his right thigh touching hers, his strong callused hands taking up the reins. He released the brake lever with a practiced motion of his left leg, and they were on their way.

He raised his hat to the small assembly of well-wishers in front of the stagecoach station, still without smiling that famous smile that had made Miranda's insides quiver, and urged the team of two mules to a faster pace with a raspy sound from his throat and a slap of the reins.

He did not look at Miranda, but kept his thoughtful gaze fixed on the track ahead. The far edges of the clearing where the town of Springwater was slowly taking shape were a fringe of gold and crimson, rust and dark green. The sky was a pristine, chilly blue, dabbed with white, and there was a quiet, thrilling sense of new beginnings, it seemed to her, woven in the air itself and into the bright, eager glow of the sun. She held her small son closer against her bosom as he began to fidget, and sat proudly beside her husband.

Her husband. Miranda let her thoughts wander back to the day the Doc and Savannah were married. There had been a party then, and dancing to the tunes of a fiddle, and she'd been Landry's partner in a reel. When that spin around the floor of the Springwater station's main room had ended, Miranda was a different woman, totally changed. She'd loved the smell of Landry Kildare from then on, loved the sight of him, and the sound of his voice.

Now, officially his wife, Miranda wanted to laugh aloud with joy, but she knew that would startle the baby and Landry, too, and maybe even the mules, so she held her exuberance inside, contained it, like a deep breath, drawn against a plunge underwater. In her mind, she rehearsed the life that lay ahead — Landry's boys would come to love her like a second mother, she'd see to that. She'd stitch curtains for every window in the house, and keep the place so clean that folks were sure to remark upon it for miles around. She wasn't the best cook — her fare tended to be plain and a little on the heavy side — but she'd learned a few things helping Miss June-bug in the Springwater station kitchen, and she'd manage just fine. With practice, she expected she'd be able to make biscuits as feathery as anybody's.

Yes, she assured herself, she would make it all work. Landry Kildare would never be sorry he'd taken her for a wife. Maybe one day, he might even come to love her, if she worked at things hard enough. It made her heart pound a little, just to imagine him looking at her the way Trey looked at Rachel, for example, or the way Doc looked at Savannah.

The ride to his home — glory of glories, it

was hers now, too, and the baby's — was short by comparison to the distance to say, the Wainwright place, or Choteau. Or Ohio, for that matter.

The thought of Ohio, and the home place where her ma was buried, took a little of the shine off that magical day, bringing the farm to mind as it did and, with it, her lost mother. Miranda set the memories firmly aside. No sense looking back, longing for places and people she would never see again. No, sir. Miranda Leebrook Kildare meant to fix her gaze straight ahead, from that moment on.

Miranda was a pretty little thing, Landry thought guiltily, as the team covered the last couple of miles, the buckboard rattling along over a rocky, rutted track. Eighteen, no more than that, and here he was, thirty-five, come next June. Nearly twice her age.

He ground his back teeth. It wasn't like he was betraying Caroline; she'd been gone a long time, and he'd been lonely enough to howl ever since. He'd never stopped loving her, not for a moment, but he'd taken some-thing of a shine to Rachel Hargreaves, when she'd come to teach at Springwater the year before. She'd been Rachel English then, spirited as a filly raised on the open range, but book-smart, too, and pretty. Alas, she'd married Trey Hargreaves, then half owner of the Brimstone Saloon, and never thought of Landry as anything more than a friend.

Just as well, he supposed, given the fact that Trey and Rachel clearly loved each other as deeply as he and Caroline ever had. Landry couldn't have offered Rachel that kind of sentiment, much as he admired her, so she was better off with the man she'd chosen.

Landry sighed to himself, and prodded the mules to travel a little faster. Maybe he'd lost his mind, waking up that morning with the intention of getting married before the day was out, but here he was, with a bride in tow, and sunset still a good four hours off.

Oh, he'd been mulling the idea over for a long while, of course. Ever since Rachel English's arrival at Springwater, anyway. Maybe before that, if he wanted to be honest with himself.

Well, in any case, the deed was done. He and Miranda were hitched, right and proper, and even though they could probably get an annulment, given that the marriage hadn't been consummated, Landry had no intention of seeking one. He'd thought the whole thing through, the way he did every new undertaking, looking at all the fors and againsts; he'd made his decision and he would abide by it.

He set his jaw.

"Mr. Kildare?"

At first, he didn't know who she was talking to; proof enough of his state of mind, he thought ruefully, given the fact that he was the only one there, besides the baby and a pair of jackasses. "You can call me Landry," he said, and for the first time since he'd opened his eyes before dawn and set his mind on getting married, he smiled. "My boys are Marcus, he's eleven, and Jamie, he's nine. I don't mind telling you, they're a handful."

Just for a moment, a shadow of uncertainty moved in her eyes. She'd met his sons, of course, Springwater being a small place. Heard tales about them, no doubt. Hell, they'd all be lucky if she didn't take to her heels before supper was set out. "How do they feel about having me and little Isaiah-or-Ezekiel around?"

Landry ran the tip of his tongue along the inside of his lower lip. "I didn't mention that I was planning to get married today," he said. "I had enough to do, just getting those little heathens off to school."

She stared at him, held her baby a little closer. "You haven't told them?"

He started to pat her knee with his free hand, then thought better of the gesture. Better not to touch her, lest he start getting ideas he didn't have any right to entertain. "Don't go fretting yourself about my boys," he said. "They'll be glad enough to eat somebody's cooking besides mine."

Miranda didn't look all that reassured. He'd have sworn she gulped, as a matter of fact, and he fully expected her to say she'd heard his boys were monsters, which, regretfully, they were. Had been, ever since their mother died. Instead, she asked, "What made you pick me? For a bride, I mean?"

They rounded the last bend, and the ranch house and barn were visible up ahead; Landry felt the same brief, skittering sensation of pride he always did when he first got a look at the place, whether he'd been away an hour or a week. All the same, he fixed his full attention on Miranda's troubled face.

"Well," he said, a forthright nature being his private curse, "you were the only unmarried woman around here."

A difficult silence settled over them, broken only by the jingle of harness fittings and the *cloppity-clop* sound of hooves.

She drew the baby close again, murmured something to him, even though he hadn't stirred or made a sound. While she spoke, her gaze was on the house, the barn and corral, the trees, though it seemed to Landry that she might have been looking past those things to some other place, some other time. "I reckon that makes about as much sense as anything," she said, in a small voice. It made him hurt, the way she straightened her spine and raised her chin. "You probably could have sent away for a wife, but that would have taken some considerable time."

He felt a stab of pity for her, but he understood pride, having an overabundance of it himself, and so did not let the emotion show. They were nearly at the gate now; he drew up on the reins, set the brake lever, and moved to jump down and raise the wooden latch. Something he'd heard in her voice, however, kept him from leaving the buckboard seat.

"You truly don't mind? About the baby, I mean?"

He had, of course, given the child a great deal of thought, and long since decided that the sins of the father — or the mother — should not be visited on the son. "You're my wife now," he said quietly, "and I expect you to be faithful to me. But whatever happened before today is your own business.

We'll go on from here."

She gave him a shaky smile that stirred something awake inside him, something that had been asleep for a long time. "You're not like most men, Landry Kildare," she said. There was a glint of shy admiration in her eyes.

He grinned that time, more because he had no answer to offer than because he was amused, and got down to let the team through. When the mules and wagon were inside the fence, he closed the gate again and climbed up beside Miranda once more, to take up the reins.

"I'll put the buckboard away," he said, "and turn the mules out to graze awhile, before I start on that field. You and the baby go on inside and make yourselves at home. I'll come in after a bit to see that you've settled in and all."

She nodded, somewhat primly he thought, and looked down at the top of the infant's head, which was hidden by the blankets. He wondered if the kid could breathe freely, swaddled up that way, but couldn't quite bring himself to ask. He brought the wagon to a halt and helped Miranda down, lifting her by the waist.

She was light, but sturdy, and strong as an otter pup. She held on to that baby like she thought he was going to snatch the little mite out of her arms and throw him down the well. When she was standing on her own two feet, he wrenched off his hat and held it out, stiff-armed as a scarecrow.

"There's the house," he said, like she couldn't see it, standing right there where he'd left it. "You can go on in."

Another woman might have laughed, or at least smiled, at his discomfiture, which must have been as obvious as that cabin or the mountains or the sky over their heads, but she didn't. She just stood there, with the last-gasp-of-summer breeze dancing through tendrils of her chestnut hair, some of which had come down from its pins during the ride out from Springwater, her eyes dark as bruises and so full of naked yearning that it nearly killed Landry just to look at her.

He averted his eyes for a moment, out of plain decency. "I'll be in after a while," he said. Then he took hold of the harness, near the lead mule's jawbone, and started off toward the barnyard. The team followed, the buckboard bouncing along behind them, flimsy without the weight of its passengers.

Miranda stood in the doorway of the Kildare house, struck by the neatness of the place. It didn't seem like a household of men, with its polished floors and sootless stone fireplace. There were curtains at the windows, crisp and new enough that they hadn't faded, and the rag rugs made splashes of color here and there, just inside the threshold, under her own feet, in front of the hearth, over by the big wood cookstove. There was a bright red-and-white checked cloth on the table, and somebody had picked a handful of dandelion ghosts and the very last of the wild tiger lilies and set them on a windowsill in a fruit jar bouquet.

It was as though the lost Caroline Kildare had just left the room, moments before; Miranda could almost catch the scent of her perfume in the air, delicate and simple, but perfume nonetheless.

She sighed and closed the door gently behind her, unwrapping her sleeping child from his many blankets. She was a bit overprotective of little Isaiah-or-Ezekiel, but it wasn't something she could help. The world was a dangerous and unpredictable place, and she'd seen countless babies die since the time she'd begun to take notice of such matters. It was important to keep him warm.

The baby began to fuss a little, weary of being held and jostled. He probably needed his diaper changed, and some nourishment as well; she remembered that her belongings were still in the buckboard and set her shoulders. Mr. Kildare — Landry — would bring everything along when he came back to the house.

Patting her son's sturdy little back, for he was starting to carry on in earnest now, Miranda went in search of whatever loft, lean-to, or nook was meant to serve as her private retreat. The first room she entered was plainly Landry's; his bed, covered by a truly magnificent quilt, was large and hand-carved, with images of horses and eagles in the headboard, his boots were lined up under a window, his spare clothes hung neatly on pegs along the shady wall.

Miranda felt a stirring she understood all too well, and slipped out.

The next room, which was as untidy as Landry's was neat, clearly belonged to the boys. There were two beds, both unmade, and little shirts and trousers spread from one end of the floor to the other.

She closed the door and proceeded to the last door. Inside, she found a slanted ceiling, a plain, narrow bed, and a comfortable chair with a stitchery basket sitting beside it on the floor. This, no doubt, had been Caroline's refuge, a place to rock her babies, to sew, to dream and think. Miranda felt an uncharitable — and uncharacteristic — pang of envy toward this unknown woman. Even though she'd been gone for several years — June-bug had said her grave was in a copse of trees nearby — Mrs. Landry Kildare was still a presence in that house.

Resigned, Miranda laid her now-squalling baby on the bed and searched until she found some old pieces of cloth in one of the bureau drawers — big squares of blue calico, probably intended for a quilt top. Having no other choice at hand, she put one to practical use, and she was sitting in the ornate rocking chair, one breast bared to nurse her baby, when she heard the cabin door open and close in the distance.

Before she could consider the immodesty of her situation any further, Landry was standing in the doorway. His stance was easy, relaxed, yet his hands looked hard where they gripped the wooden framework on either side of him, and his gaze lingered a moment too long on her breast before shooting up to her face.

"I brought your things in from the wagon," he said, awkwardly, and after a long time had passed.

Miranda was embarrassed, for all that it was an ordinary thing to breast-feed a baby, and the suckling sound seemed to echo off the cabin walls. She wanted to cover her burning face, not to mention her naked bosom, but the only way she could have done that without disturbing the baby would be to pull her skirts up over her head, which was, of course, no sort of solution. Still, she knew her discomfiture showed, knew by the heat in her flesh and the anxious leap in the pit of her stomach. "Thank you," she said.

He stared at her for a few moments longer, looking hard at her face, and then thrust himself forward and into the room with a small action of his powerful arms. Going to the bureau, he rooted around and found a lacy crocheted blanket, infant-size, which he draped over her and the baby with a motion so gentle that it tugged at a tiny muscle in the back of Miranda's throat. His was a simple, earthy sort of tenderness, nothing she ought to take meaning from, she knew, and yet she set store by it, even prized it. That particular brand of kindness had been sorely lacking in her experience.

She thought Landry would leave then, but instead he sat down on the edge of that narrow bed, the springs creaking beneath him. He looked around the small room as though he hadn't been inside it in years, and maybe he hadn't, though it showed the same degree of neatness as most of the house did. "Caroline used to sew in here," he said, with a sigh that conveyed humor, rather than sorrow, and was somehow, therefore, all the more poignant. "She said it made her feel like she was living in a mansion, having a whole room to herself when she wanted some peace and quiet."

Miranda smiled because he was smiling, but deep down, and for a reason she could not put a name to, she would rather have wept. "I reckon I would have liked her a lot," she said, and it was true, for all that she wished, in that moment, that the other woman had never existed. That, somehow, she could have managed to be first in someone's life, rather than a mere afterthought, a person who barely sufficed, except as a substitute.

He expelled his breath in a combination laugh and chuckle, a sound, Miranda would soon realize, that was uniquely his, like so many other qualities she saw in him.

"Speak up if you need anything," he said, and hoisted himself to his feet. Sure enough, the old satchel Miss June-bug had given her the loan of was sitting just inside the doorway, with the bundle of diapers and blankets and little baby clothes packed away inside. "I'll get you some water for washing up, if you'd like."

She nodded, biting her lower lip. She was absurdly grateful, maybe because no man had ever treated her with such courtesy, not even the one who'd persuaded her to lie down beside him, to surrender her innocence, and then left her, pregnant with his child. Tears sprang to her eyes; she nodded once more and turned her head, hoping Landry wouldn't see, wouldn't question her.

He did both. He caught her chin in his gentle, callused grip, and raised her face, looked full on at her sorrow and didn't flinch. "You'll have no call to fear me," he said. "I promise you that."

"I ain't — *I'm not* afraid of you," she sniffled, patting the baby as he let go of her nipple under the faintly musty infant's blanket and fell headlong into a sated, milky sleep. "I just — well — a lot's changed for me just since I got out of bed this morning. I don't rightly know what to make of it all."

He drew back, and she was sorry for that; she experienced the withdrawal of his hand as a tearing-away. "You've got plenty of time to sort things through," he said quietly, and though his expression was serious, there was a certain tender mischief dancing in his eyes. "I'll get that water for you," he reiterated, and then he was gone.

Miranda fastened her bodice and laid little Isaiah-or-Ezekiel on the bed, with a pillow propped on either side to keep him from rolling off onto the floor. He slept contentedly, his long pale lashes lying like gilded fans on his cheeks. Just looking at him made her feel better.

She was taken by surprise when Landry appeared with a basin in one hand and a bucket in the other, and started a little. He was looking at her in that strange, thoughtful way again, as though he'd never seen a woman with a baby before. Or, she reflected, a moment later, as if he hadn't seen one in a very long while.

"Thank you," she said, pretending she was Rachel Hargreaves. She did that sometimes when she was scared, or overwhelmed, which was a good bit of the time. Made believe she was somebody else, most often Rachel or Savannah. It was a childish game, she knew, and by rights she ought to give it up, but she hadn't quite been able to let it go.

Landry set the basin on the bureau top, the bucket on the floor beside it. Inside the basin, he'd set a bar of soap and a square of clean cloth.

"I'd best get back to work," he said, in that same hoarse voice he'd used to ask for her hand in marriage earlier that day. "The boys will be home from school long about four — you tell 'em I'll tan their hides if they don't put that room of theirs to rights. I'll carry my dinner out to the fields and come in for supper by sundown."

Miranda could only nod yet again. She'd contrive to have something ready for him to eat even if she died in the effort, she promised herself. She wasn't so sure of her ability to deal with Marcus and Jamie, though. They were a pair of red-haired terrors, those boys, and even pretending to be Rachel probably wouldn't be enough to buffalo them into minding her. Then again, if she didn't get the upper hand right away, they'd surely make her life a pure and certain misery.

"I'll be looking for you to come in after the work is done," Miranda said, belatedly realizing that Landry was waiting for an answer to his statement, or at least an acknowledgment.

"You'll find canned goods and the like in the pantry," he said, as if reluctant to go, "and milk and butter out in the spring-house. We've got chickens and a cow, and once I get the butchering done, there'll be ham, too. I could show you —"

Miranda squared her shoulders. She couldn't have him thinking he'd tied himself to somebody helpless. "I reckon I can manage," she said.

He nodded, made a parting gesture with the hand that still held his hat, and went out. Miranda immediately washed her face and hands, tidied up her hair, and then rummaged through the bureau again, until she found a pretty gingham apron to tie around her waist.

She was peeling plump, smooth-skinned potatoes when the boys burst into the house, moving fit to outrun their own skins. Seeing Miranda working by the stove, they stared at her with round blue eyes, and it seemed their freckles might just leap right off their faces.

"By gum, it's true," marveled the taller of the two. That would be Jamie, Miranda knew. Although he was younger than his brother, he was the bigger one.

"Pa took himself a wife, just like Toby said!" Marcus added.

Miranda couldn't tell whether her new stepsons were delighted or outraged, and she pretended not to care one way or the other. "I imagine you're hungry," she said. "Learning taxes a body. You'll find some molasses cookies there in the pantry."

She'd used June-bug's recipe to bake those cookies, stirring in a generous portion of bravado. The boys' response to the offering was important to her, but she didn't dare let them know. Rachel wouldn't show her hand like that so early in the game, and neither would Savannah.

They rushed the pantry, those boys, like soldiers taking an enemy fort by storm, and came out with cookies in either hand.

"Where's Pa?" demanded Marcus.

"Why did he pick you?" Jamie added, face squenched with confusion.

Miranda held her ground, didn't let on for a moment that she was nervous. "Your pa is where he usually is, at this time of the day — working. He said you're to clean up your room or he'll tan your hides for sure. And I reckon he picked me because he thought I'd do as well as anybody else."

The boys just stared at her for what seemed like a long while; they were handsome lads, she thought, with a sort of pride. They'd grow up to be fine men, if she had anything to say about it. Oh, yes, she thought, with new resolve, if she could give Landry nothing else, she would give him a mother for his sons.

Jamie looked her up and down. "You ain't

hardly any older than Marcus here," he said.

"I'm eighteen," Miranda said. "And I've got a baby."

"You weren't married when you got him, neither," observed Marcus.

"I know," Miranda answered reasonably. Calmly. But inside, she felt like a deer on ice.

"You're supposed to be married if you mean to have babies," Marcus informed her.

Jamie assessed her again, thoughtfully, this time, and quite without rancor. "Are you and Pa going to make any? Babies, I mean?"

She swallowed. "I reckon," she allowed.

"Well," Jamie retorted, "if you do, see that you just have boys. The last thing we need around here is a passel of squalling *girls*."

Miranda smiled. She hadn't had time to think about bearing Landry's child, not since marrying him anyway, but now that it was in her mind, she found she liked the idea. "I think it would be nice to have a girl. Somebody to keep me company." She had no more than drawn her next breath after saying those words when Landry filled the gaping space in the doorway.

It was plain from the expression on his face that he'd heard what she said, and he had thoughts of his own about making babies.

2

Landry watched, intrigued, as his new bride, seated across the supper table from him, dished up a plate of cornbread and beans for him, then one for each of the boys, before serving herself. Her thick brown hair was pinned up at her nape in a lopsided, wifely do, with a few tendrils straggling down here and there around her cheeks and temples and one side of her neck. Her good skin seemed to glow in the light from the lamps and the fireplace, and her dark blue eyes were bright. She seemed surprisingly happy to Landry, given the fact that she'd married a virtual stranger just that morning.

The baby, little Isaiah-or-Ezekiel, whom Landry already thought of as "Little One-or-the-other," cooed cheerfully nearby, cosseted in Caroline's wicker laundry basket. Landry felt a muscle tighten in his jaw. Caroline's house, Caroline's pots and pans, Caroline's children, Caroline's husband.

How long would it be, he wondered, before he got used to seeing this strange and lovely woman-child filling places that rightfully belonged to his first and only love?

As if she felt his gaze, Miranda glanced at him and flushed in the lamplight. She looked as innocent as an angel, sitting there, hair and skin and eyes all shining, but she wasn't any such thing, he reminded himself sternly. She was a fallen woman, and that was one of the reasons he'd decided to marry her. There would be no danger of his caring too much for somebody he couldn't respect. No threat to Caroline's memory.

"Is everything all right?" Miranda asked, her brow puckering a little, but prettily. Damn, but he hadn't realized she was so fetching — had he?

The boys were eating, mannerly as a couple of Jesuits fresh from some Eastern seminary. He wondered what *that* was about, even as he swallowed hard, feeling oddly guilty, and rummaged through his mind for an answer to her perfectly ordinary, perfectly simple question.

"Fine," he said, at some length. Now *there*, he chided himself, was an intelligent reply. Maybe he was never going to love this young woman, but if she was going to live with him for the next however-many years, she'd be likely to expect more in the way of conversation. Women were that way — even Caroline, sanctified by his memory into something resembling a saint, had wanted to talk from the moment he stepped over the threshold after a day's work, straight on through supper and half the night, if he let her. It was as if they stored up their words all day, these females, and then unleashed them in a frightening torrent at the first sight of a man.

Marcus leaped into the breach just then, bless his skinned knees and mismatched socks. "We ought to call that baby something in particular," he said, gazing thoughtfully toward the gurgling infant waving both hands and both feet in the depths of the washbasket. "What's he need with two names, anyhow?"

"Let's call him Rover," Jamie suggested.

Landry sucked in a snicker at that, and saw Miranda schooling a smile of her own. She even managed to look like she was considering the idea carefully before reluctantly ruling it out with a shake of her head. "He has a name. Isaiah —" she paused and frowned. "Or Ezekiel."

"Rover's a dog's name, stupid," Marcus informed his brother. Though he was the elder of the pair, he was usually a beat behind Jamie. It worried Landry a little some-times. "He ain't a dog."

"Isn't," Landry corrected his son automati-cally. He'd picked the habit up from Caro-line and never gotten away from it, even after her passing. If she'd wanted one thing in the world, Caroline had, it was for those rapscallion boys of theirs to grow up into decent, hardworking, mannerly men. As far as Landry could see, there wasn't a whole lot of progress being made toward that end.

"How about George?" Jamie suggested. They were studying history in school, Lan-dry knew, and the boy was probably think-ing of the country's first president.

Miranda smiled at Landry, with her eyes, and continued to eat, without comment. She took small, delicate bites, despite the obvious fact that she'd been raised rough-and-tumble, and something about the way she moved, the way she held her head and shoulders, stirred him on a deep and very private level. He didn't want to let her or any other woman into that place inside him, where he'd set up a shrine to Caroline.

"George," scoffed Marcus.

"Enough," Landry interjected quietly. "It's Miranda's place to decide on the baby's name, not yours."

"Where's that baby's pa, anyway?"

Jamie asked bluntly.

Miranda stiffened, but only for a fraction of a second. Not surprisingly, she'd had a good deal of practice where that inquiry was concerned. "I don't rightly know," she said. "Somewhere between St. Louis and Laramie, I reckon." For an instant there was a bruised expression in those near-purple eyes of hers that nearly closed off Landry's throat.

That was why it took him a moment too long to intercede. "Jamie," he said, "there are certain things you just don't say to people. One more step in that direction, and you'll leave the table."

Jamie flushed with righteous indignation, but he backed down. Landry, for all that he'd set his son straight on the issue, wondered himself about the man who had charmed Miranda into a mistake that might well have ruined her life, and wondered mightily. Maybe at some point, when she'd had time to settle into the household, he'd just haul off and ask her. In private, of course.

After that, Miranda seemed to lose her appetite. She left the table and scraped the remains of her supper into the scrap bucket by the stove, a wooden one reserved for slopping the hogs. Her shoulders were especially straight, almost to the point of rigidity, and Landry thought he heard her sniffle once or twice. The baby, as if sensing his mother's discomfort, began to fret and fuss.

"Sit down a spell, Miranda," Landry told his bride evenly, but in a tone meant to convey that he was giving an order, not making a request. "The boys will do up the dishes."

Amid wails of protest from Jamie and Marcus, Miranda stood stock still, plate still in hand, staring at Landry as if he'd told her to build a room onto the house before morning. He knew all too little about her, but it wasn't hard to deduce that she was used to doing all the "women's work" that needed to be done.

The baby began to holler, tiny fists knotted, feet pummeling the air. He had gumption, that kid, Landry thought, with a peculiar sort of pride. He hadn't fathered Little One-or-the-other, but he was already getting attached. He liked kids, especially the really small ones that didn't give you much guff.

Biting her lip, Miranda finally nodded in acquiescence, put aside the plate, and crossed the plank floor to lift her child from his basket and prop him against one shoulder, murmuring and patting his back. He was hungry, Little One-or-the-other, and Miranda was already headed toward the privacy of the spare room, in order to nurse him.

The thought of that tightened Landry's groin; in order to distract himself, he fixed his attention on his squabbling sons. "Get on with it," he said, nodding toward the metal sink.

Grumbling, the boys cleared the table, scraped their plates, and began scooping hot water out of the stove reservoir to fill the sink. Landry got his cherrywood pipe from the mantel, along with a match and a pouch of his best tobacco. He was no longer a widower, but somebody's husband, he reflected, marveling at the changes one decision, one day, could make in a man's life.

Outside, he filled the pipe, struck a match off the heavy door frame, and tried his level best to concentrate on smoking.

Jehosaphat. He was married.

There was a woman living under his roof now, a stepmother for his boys, a companion, of sorts, for him. He couldn't help thinking of her, there in the spare room, with one well-shaped breast bared to suckle the baby, and stopped trying to deny that he wanted a wedding night, wanted Miranda. He'd have done better, he reprimanded himself, to find himself an ugly woman. What had possessed him to choose one who was young and pretty and, well, plainly receptive to the intimate attentions of a man?

He made himself remember Caroline. She hadn't cared much for the private aspects of marriage, he had to admit, though she'd accommodated him willingly enough whenever he turned to her in the night.

Irritated, for a reason he couldn't precisely define, he thrust himself away from the support pole he'd been leaning against and strode off into the darkness. He'd make a pilgrimage to Caroline's grave, sit there awhile in the dry autumn grass, and go through his memories of her one by one, feeling the shape and weight of each, like a man fingering holy beads.

He hadn't consciously planned to pass the spare room window, but he did, and he glanced in, too. Miranda was there, all right, seated in the soft glow of a single lamp, unaware of him, looking down at her suckling baby with an expression of such tender devotion that Landry's eyes burned a little. He blinked and looked away.

"Damn," he muttered. The night seemed almost solid after that; it settled over him like a dark blanket. He went on toward Caroline's final resting place, crossing the creek at a narrow place and heading for the copse of birches, alders, and cottonwoods that surrounded the fine wood cross he'd carved for her, working on it throughout that first long, impossible winter after her passing.

"I got married today," he said, as soon as he got near enough. The fall wind was chilly; he felt it through his shirt. "I know you'll understand, if there's a way you can hear me." He thrust one hand through his hair; he'd forgotten his hat, in his haste to get out of the house and away from his new bride. "I don't love her, Caroline. Hell, I don't hardly know her. But the boys have been running wild ever since you left us and I — well, sometimes I get so lonesome, I fear to die of it."

There was no answer, of course; just the whisper of the wind in the tree branches, the rustling of leaves as small woodland creatures went about their business, and the steady murmur of the creek. It usually made Landry feel better, at least marginally, if he came out here and told Caroline what was on his heart, but somehow tonight was different. He was more aware than ever that Caroline had long since gone on to some other, ostensibly better place, and left him behind.

He crouched beside the creek, tapped out his pipe on a smooth, damp stone. He'd made a mistake in taking a new wife, he thought now, with rueful certainty. That was the reason he'd lost the precious sense of reaching out to Caroline, finding her there in the mystery just beyond what he could see or hear or touch.

He sighed, raised himself to his full height again, and tucked the pipe into his shirt pocket, alongside the tobacco pouch. "I don't reckon I'll be spending as much time here, after this," he said quietly, though whether he was addressing himself, God, or the surrounding countryside, he didn't know. The sense of loss was profound, aching in every part of him, settling into the very marrow of his bones.

He went to the barn, even though he'd already done all the evening chores, to check on the livestock. He was a prosperous man, thanks to years of single-minded hard work and prudence, and he'd doubled the size of his holdings a year before by buying up Trey Hargreaves's homestead. He had healthy sons, friends aplenty, a good house, land and livestock, cash money stashed in the safe at the Springwater station and in a lard can hidden beneath a floorboard in the toolshed. Everything that was supposed to make him happy — except for a woman he truly loved.

Oh, Miranda would sit next to him when Jacob McCaffrey preached of a Sunday, she'd probably even share his bed if he asked it of her. But it wouldn't be the same. He was, he reasoned, as lonely as he'd ever been — maybe more so, because he didn't even have the consolation of bedding this wife he'd taken on what seemed a foolish impulse.

Presently, resigned, he returned to the house.

The boys had finished washing the dishes, in their haphazard way, and were seated at the table again, bent over their slates. Miranda, holding the baby on one well-rounded hip, was supervising.

"Is that the right way to spell 'legislature'?" Jamie asked, holding up his slate for her to see.

Her gaze had connected with Landry's as soon as he stepped through the doorway, then skittered away. Now, she bit her lower lip and narrowed her eyes. There was a slight flush on her cheekbones.

"I don't reckon I know," she said, at some length, with a note of soft misery in her voice.

Landry shut and latched the door,

crossed to the table, looked over his son's shoulder at the word scrawled across the small chalkboard. "Try again," he advised, and glanced up at Miranda.

She turned away quickly, busied herself tucking the baby back into Caroline's basket. Her embarrassment was almost palpable, all the same, and Landry felt a stab of something resembling pity. He wondered if she could read at all, or if she simply had difficulty deciphering long words. One thing was certain: it would only make matters worse if he asked her about it in front of the boys.

In good time, and under violent protest, Jamie and Marcus washed their faces and their teeth at the washstand by the fireplace, then took themselves off to bed. Landry watched them go with a feeling of fond good humor, standing with one elbow braced against the mantelpiece, his pipe and tobacco in the opposite hand.

"You aren't going to smoke, are you?" Miranda asked. He saw it then, the first spark of challenge he'd ever glimpsed in her. She *did* have a certain spirit, he thought, and was pleased.

Still, the inquiry itself surprised him. In the first place, he hadn't expected her to speak up so firmly, she'd seemed so shy around him. In the second, this was his house and he'd smoke if he damned well wanted to. It was just that he didn't happen to want to, that was all — he'd only taken the pipe and tobacco from his shirt pocket so he could put them in the cigar box on the shelf over the hearth, where they belonged.

Landry put the items away with pointed motions, and the lid of the cigar box closed with a little *slap*. "Are you against tobacco?" he asked, in a tone just this side of annoyance.

She glanced at the baby, now sleeping soundly in his improvised bed. "It makes the air bad," she said nervously, but with conviction. "I don't much cotton to drinking, either. You don't take liquor, do you?"

Landry rarely indulged — he simply didn't like the taste of wine or whiskey — but it was the principle of the thing. "I do my smoking outside," he allowed quietly, evenly, not wanting the boys to overhear, "and I'm not fond of spirits in general, but I'm the head of this household and I wear the pants. I'll thank you to remember that, Mrs. Kildare."

She looked surprised that he'd called her that; he was a little off-balance himself. *Caroline* was "Mrs. Kildare," he thought.

Miranda was merely, well, Miranda. She started to say something, then knotted her hands in the apron she'd probably appropriated from the bureau in the spare room and held her tongue.

He looked her up and down, assessingly, without desire or any other emotion. He told himself that what he felt was cool detachment and wondered at one and the same time when he'd come to find lying so easy. "Do you know how to sew?" he asked, after clearing his throat once. It was a rare woman who wasn't handy with a needle and thread, in Landry's experience, but Miranda was not the usual sort of female.

She swallowed. "I can mend," she said, sounding a mite defensive. "I can darn socks, too. I can do the wash and use a flatiron and make soap. I can hoe and weed and slop pigs and chase down lost cows —"

He almost chuckled at her earnest expression, but stopped himself just in time. God knew, he was no hand with the ladies, having married Caroline right out of school, after living on the next farm from her father's place virtually all his life, but he knew better than to laugh at a woman. That was straight-out asking for trouble, even when you didn't mean anything by it.

"What I meant was, you'll be wanting

some dresses and the like." He was afraid he might have reddened a little, just to touch on the subject of the fripperies women wore beneath their everyday clothes. Caroline had liked to wear lace, and ribbon, too, though they were hard to come by, so far from a big city. "I reckoned you could make them."

She looked almost wretched. "Well, I ain't — I'm not very good at such. I could manage dresses and petticoats, I figure, but drawers and camisoles take a fine hand —"

Now it was Landry who swallowed. Drawers and camisoles? Dear God. "Maybe June-bug McCaffrey would be willing to teach you," he said, and the words came out sounding like bits of rusted metal run through a grinder. "I should have the hogs butchered and strung up in the smokehouse in a week or ten days. We'll take the stage into Choteau and get whatever you want."

Her eyes widened. "You mean, you're going to *buy* things? Brand new?"

He smiled. "That's what I mean, all right. You'll be wanting yard goods — something heavy to make a cloak, too. It gets right cold around here, long about the end of October." He paused thoughtfully, glad of a mental errand to take his mind off things he oughtn't to think about. "Those shoes won't last another season," he decided aloud, looking at her feet. It should be safe, looking at her feet, since he couldn't see her ankles or anything. "We'll get you some sturdy boots for when the snows come, and a pair of high-buttons to wear to church."

That fetching color bloomed on her cheeks again, turning them pink as wild sweetbriar blossoms. "I can make do with what I've got," she said. "I been doin' that for as long as I can remember."

He wanted, not so suddenly, to touch her, even if it was only to cup that proud little chin of hers in one hand, but he didn't dare. He was on the verge of sweeping her up in his arms and carrying her off to his bed as it was, and he had given his word that she'd have ample time to get used to living in a new place, with new people all around her. He was not a man to go back on his promises.

"I don't plan to buy out the stores, Miranda," he pointed out, with a gentleness he hadn't known was in him. No, he'd wanted to present himself as matter-of-fact, even stern. Head of the household, wearing the pants, making the decisions, etc. "We'll just get a few things. Maybe some knickers for little —" he'd been about to say One-or-the-other, but he caught himself just in

47

time, "for the baby, there."

She blinked, pressed one splay-fingered hand to her bosom, and sank into a chair at the table, as though overcome. "Well, don't that beat everything?" she murmured.

"*Doesn't,*" Landry corrected, and started into his nightly routine of lowering the door latch, shuttering the windows, turning down the damper in the stove, banking the fire. When he thought to look toward her chair again, Miranda was gone.

She sat on the edge of the narrow bed, both hands pressed to her cheeks, which were as hot as if she'd taken a fever, and tried to stop her mind from spinning. She'd carried the baby's basket-bed along with her when she left the main room, and little Isaiah-or-Ezekiel was sleeping as peacefully as if his mother's life, and therefore his own, hadn't been turned upside down and shaken loose, just since the sun rose that morning.

Miranda had kept house for her father following her mother's passing, and she'd waited on him afterwards, too. Not once had he ever offered so much as a ribbon for her hair — even though she'd once prayed for a strand of blue grosgrain for a solid six months — let alone suggested going into a real store and laying down cash money for woman things. Miranda had been clothing herself in hand-me-downs and cast-offs for as long as she could remember — even when her ma was living, and sewing when she could, there usually hadn't been money for yard goods. The garments Mrs. McCaffrey and Rachel and Savannah had given her since her arrival in Springwater showed barely any wear. She was grateful for them, and hadn't imagined having anything better. Anything made just for her.

The concept was almost frightening, and she rocked slightly back and forth, trying to calm herself and gather in her scattered thoughts. It was bad enough that Landry was so handsome, that just looking at him always left an aching thumbprint on her heart. If he was going to be generous on top of it all, well, she didn't for sure know what she'd do. Did he expect something from her, besides the things he'd outlined when he'd proposed to her back at Springwater? Would he come to the spare room in the night, to lie with her, or look for her to come to him?

She recollected how it was before, giving herself to a man, lying in the tall grass, with the stars scattered all across the sky like a spill of crystal beads and the breeze washing over her bare flesh, cool and smelling of prairie wildflowers . . .

Miranda closed her eyes tight and hugged herself harder, but it didn't help. She remembered being taken, remembered it all too clearly. It hadn't been pleasant, the way Evangeline and Rachel and Savannah all hinted that such things were supposed to be, not at all. She'd merely endured, and listened to him whisper pretty words that she'd guessed, even then, were lies. Still, to someone as starved for affection as Miranda had been, lies notwithstanding, the trade was worthwhile.

Landry, now, he made her feel entirely different about the whole subject. Ever since she'd first glimpsed him, not long after her arrival at Springwater, in fact, she'd dreamed about lying down with him. Hadn't been able to *help* imagining what it would be like if it were Landry who unbuttoned her dress, loosed the ribbons of her camisole, bared her breasts, lifted her skirts —

She moaned aloud. *Stop,* she commanded herself. *Stop thinking about that, stop thinking about him!*

It did no good at all, giving herself such an order. Her mind, her body, even her soul, were full to bursting of Landry Kildare.

A rap at her door startled her so badly that she actually gasped aloud. "Y-yes?" she called, when she'd reined in her runaway breath.

Landry's voice came through the door, pitched low, but with no effort at persuasion. "I forgot to ask if you needed to go outside. If you're afraid, I'll walk with you."

Miranda closed her eyes again, tighter than ever, and realized that her bladder was painfully full. "No, thanks," she chimed, in what she hoped was a cheerful and offhand tone. She'd die of mortification, sitting there in the privy, relieving herself, with Landry standing guard right outside the door. "I'll just take a lamp."

He hesitated, then bid her good-night. She heard him walking away. When the sound of his door closing reached her ears, she jumped up, grabbed the kerosene lantern on her bedside table, and hurried through the house. She was back in the darkened main room of the cabin, washing her hands and face at the basin, before she realized that Landry was in the room, still fully clothed except for his boots and seated in a chair before the hearth.

She started again. "I didn't see you," she said.

He didn't answer for a long while, but

simply stared into the embers in the grate. "Five years," he mused aloud, without so much as glancing her way. "This March, it'll be five years since Caroline died."

Miranda didn't bear any ill feelings toward the dead woman; in fact, she felt a certain odd kinship with her. It was indeed a tragedy for a young wife and mother to pass over before her time the way Caroline had. Still, Miranda was glad to be the one to take her place — after a fashion.

Without thinking it through first, she moved to stand behind Landry's chair and laid a hand lightly on his shoulder. He jerked, as though she'd touched his flesh with a flat-iron fresh off a hot stove, and just when she was afraid he would thrust her arm aside, he reached up instead, and laid his own hand over hers.

"Who was he?" he asked. His voice was quiet, and there was no rancor in his tone. None of the judgment and contempt that had been forthcoming from so many other people before she got to Springwater.

He was asking about the baby's father, of course, and she supposed he had a right to know, being her legal husband and all. She removed her hand from under his and came around to face him, seating herself on the apple box he used for a footstool. She stared into the fire awhile, arms wrapped around her knees.

"We came west with a wagon train. Tom was the scout — he knew the terrain and Indian habits and the like from being a sergeant in the cavalry. He told me he loved me, and that we'd be married as soon as we got as far as Laramie, and I believed him. We made a baby."

"Does he know? About his son, I mean?" Landry's voice revealed no emotion at all, and she didn't dare look at his face just then. She doubted she could have read his expression if she had, since she'd turned down the lantern when she came in from the privy, and it was dark in the room, except for the faint glow of the dying fire.

She thought a long time, debating whether or not she ought to answer, then gave a brisk, reluctant nod. "He said I must have been with somebody else, because he and his wife had tried to have children for the better part of ten years and never had any luck. That was the first time I knew he *had* a wife." She paused, blinked hard, and swallowed. After all that time, she still felt the sting of Tom's rebuff. "She had a millinery shop in Laramie," she added, for no particular reason. "It was all her own, too. Her name was Katherine."

"You met her?" Just the faintest trace of surprise in his voice, but still no verdict on her morals, one way or the other.

"I didn't actually meet her, to shake hands and the like. I was in our wagon, holding the reins while Pa was in the livery stable, trying to swap our oxen for a couple of horses, and I saw her then. She came running out of that shop when Tom rode in behind the last of the wagons, and her face was shining fit to shame the moon. When he caught sight of her, he broke into a smile and hauled her right up onto the horse with him, kissed her right there in front of the whole town."

"I'm sorry," Landry said, in his own good time.

Miranda sighed. She didn't regret bringing little Isaiah-or-Ezekiel into the world. Never that. All the same, she wished she hadn't made a fool of herself, not to mention an adulteress. "So am I," she replied softly, still watching the bright orange coals in the fireplace. "So am I."

3

First thing the next morning, Landry commenced to slaughtering and butchering the hogs. Miranda reckoned she'd be called upon to help him, and she dreaded that whole-heartedly, being that bloodshed — animal *or* human — always made her swoony, but he left the house at sunup, having made his own breakfast without so much as a rap on her door to awaken her.

She'd nursed the baby hastily, sleepily, then washed and dressed and poured herself a cup of Landry's coffee by the time the boys straggled out of their room, still in long johns, looking rumpled and none-too-amiable. They had obviously forgotten their new stepmother; when they caught sight of her, they high-tailed it back where they'd come from. When they returned, wearing pants and shirts, if not shoes, Miranda was already frying eggs and salt pork to feed them.

They ate a pile of food between them, and seemed glad enough to go off to school. The alternative would have been to help their father with the pigs, so they probably considered themselves lucky. Miranda's own pa would have made her stay home and work right alongside him.

She dallied as long as she could, cleaning up the breakfast dishes, sweeping the floor and the hearth, making up her and the boys' beds. She couldn't quite bring herself to step over the threshold of Landry's room again, but she figured he'd probably already tidied the place anyway. He was that sort of man, and Miranda couldn't rightly recall ever knowing another one quite like him.

Even Jacob McCaffrey, a man she looked up to and had come to love like a father, didn't cook for himself, sweep floors, or spread up the beds. He expected June-bug to do that kind of work, and she did, without seeming to mind. Mrs. McCaffrey had been known to aid her husband by pitching hay, too, as well as milking cows and even shoeing horses, and nobody, most especially Miranda, thought it unusual. It was just the way of things.

Now, standing inside the solid, tidy house to which she'd come as a bride less than twenty-four hours before, Miranda braced herself to be summoned to the hog pen. When considerable time had passed, with no word from Landry, she made a sling to carry little Isaiah-or-Ezekiel against her chest and set out, ready to work.

The hog pen, boasting six sows and a boar just the night before, was empty, and there was no sound of pigs squealing, no sign of the spilled blood and gore typical of such an enterprise. In fact, the whole place seemed eerily quiet.

"Landry?" she called out, in a tentative voice, raised only high enough to carry.

He appeared in the doorway of the smokehouse, crimson from the middle of his chest to his feet. He did not look pleased at the interruption, though he was, as usual, mannerly. "What is it?"

Miranda swayed as the crisp fall breeze brought the coppery scent of blood to her nostrils, mingled with the pleasant scents of dried leaves and wood smoke. "I was just — just wondering if you wanted me to — to help —"

Landry looked at her curiously. "Are you all right?"

She was, in fact, woozy. Only the fact that her baby would fall with her if she went down kept her on her feet. "I don't much like — b-blood."

His expression was eloquently ironic. "It's not my favorite part of raising pigs," he agreed, in dry tones. "You go ahead in the house and find Caroline's — find the big kettle, the one we use for laundry and making soap and the like. Carry it outside, fill it with water, and build a fire under it. You can boil up a couple of the heads while I finish hanging these critters up to cure."

Miranda gulped and turned blindly away. She was infinitely relieved to be spared the slaughtering and butchering, and she didn't let herself think as far as "boiling up a couple of the heads." She'd get through this challenge hand-over-hand, she told herself, a moment at a time if necessary.

The kettle Landry had mentioned turned out to be more of a cauldron, made of solid iron, and after several attempts at lifting the thing, she finally turned it onto its side and rolled it across the floor and over the threshold, into the front yard. She built the fire, as instructed, after fetching kindling and wood from the appropriate shed, and began lugging water from the outside pump to fill it. On about the fourth trip, with the weight of a bucket pulling either shoulder halfway out of its socket, she began to wish she'd built the fire closer to the well.

She'd just gotten the kettle to a nice

rolling boil, and she was damp with sweat from hairline to toenail with the effort, when Landry appeared, carrying something big and bloody in both arms. He flung it into the pot with a resounding splash, and headed back toward the smokehouse with no more than a nod to Miranda.

She used an old broom handle to stir the grisly contents of the kettle, and kept herself half turned away. All the same, she saw Landry approaching with another horrendous burden out of the corner of her eye, winced when she heard a second splash.

"Miranda."

She couldn't look at him, didn't dare. "W-what?"

"You don't have to stand here the whole time those heads are boiling down, chilling yourself and that baby to the bone. Just come out and make sure the fire's going once in a while. Maybe pour on some more water."

She stiffened her backbone and nodded, careful to keep her chin high. Fact was, she wanted to break down and weep with gratitude and relief. "You'll be coming in for dinner after a spell?" she asked, with a spindly effort at good cheer.

"Not like this," Landry said. "I'll strip off these duds down by the creek when I'm finished and sluice myself off as well as I can. You might bring out a plate around noon, though. Just set it on that crate outside the smokehouse door. Bring me some fresh clothes, too, while you're at it."

Miranda's face was hot as the bottom of that iron cauldron, and the heat had nothing whatsoever to do with the crackling fire or the steam off the boiling water. Her mind had gotten snagged on the image of Landry taking off his clothes by the creek, and she'd barely heard anything he said after that. Maybe her pa had been right, she thought, thoroughly chagrined. Maybe she *was* just plain no good, through and through.

She nodded rapidly, dropped the stirring stick, and hurried into the cabin. The baby was hungry again, and fussy, so she fed him, changed his diaper, and laid him down in the basket to sleep. After that, she washed her hands and face and tried to neaten her sagging, steam-dampened hair a little.

Soon, she was making biscuits, the way June-bug McCaffrey had showed her back at Springwater and sorting through the pantry for canned meat and vegetables. She made a stew from a mixture of preserved venison, carrots from a sealed jar, and onions, chopped real fine.

Within an hour, the house smelled of

home cooking, though she could still catch the underlying scent of boiled hog-head, wafting up from her dress and permeating her hair. She went outside periodically, to add wood to the fire and water to the cauldron, all without once looking into the brew, and when the sun reached the middle of the sky, she figured it was time to carry a meal to Landry.

The idea of it filled her with pleasure. She washed again, spruced her hair again, and then squared her shoulders and marched right into Landry's bedroom to fetch the fresh clothes he'd requested earlier.

The window was open, lace curtain fluttering in the breeze, and the bed, to her surprise, was unmade. Even from the doorway, Miranda could catch the clean, sun-dried laundry scent of Landry, clinging to the sheets and floating through the air itself. She found the clothes, trousers and a clean shirt, stockings and another pair of boots, a lightweight set of long underwear, stacked all of them into a neat pile, and started out of the room. She intended to come back later and smooth out the bed.

As she was turning away, however, she saw the small, ornate picture frame propped on the night table, alongside a lamp and a book resting open on its spine. Knowing all the while that she shouldn't pry, she moved toward the item that had drawn her attention, picked it up in one slightly tremulous hand.

It was a photographic likeness, oval in shape and faded with the passage of time, showing Landry and Caroline Kildare on what was presumably their wedding day. She stood behind his chair, a slender, fair-haired woman, with finely made features and the hint of a smile in her eyes, one hand resting on her husband's shoulder. Landry, seated and sober, as was the fashion, looked as though he was barely suppressing an exuberant shout, maybe of joy, maybe of triumph.

Miranda felt a distinct pang, looking at the two of them, so happy, neither suspecting how short their time together would turn out to be. She set the picture down, after a few moments, and turned away from it, mentally as well as physically, by sheer force of will. As she left Landry's bedroom, carrying his clean clothes, she was wondering where Jamie and Marcus had gotten their bright red hair. Certainly not from their father or from the blond Caroline.

She couldn't help thinking about Caroline as she made the first trip to the door of the smokehouse, where she set a full plate on the upturned wooden box, covered with a pie tin. It was gone, moments later, when she returned with the stack of clothing. She hesitated a moment, there on the other side of the high threshold from her new husband, but in the end she could not make herself step inside. She doubted, in fact, that she would be able to eat pork ever again.

After going back to the cabin once more, to make sure the baby was safe, and still sleeping soundly, she went out to add wood to the fire in the dooryard, and water to the kettle. Then, with her mind still on Caroline, she made for the copse of trees on the far side of the creek, where she knew the other woman was buried.

The grave was some distance from the stream, but she found it unerringly. It was marked by the most beautifully carved wooden cross she had ever seen — mahogany, unless she was mistaken. Where had Landry gotten mahogany, there in the wilds of Montana, where the trees were mostly pine and Douglas fir, cottonwood and cedar and birch?

He'd carved Caroline's full name into the marker, and surrounded it with delicately wrought flowers and vines. There were even birds, perched here and there among the foliage, and Miranda touched it with a feeling of wonder. It was, this sad creation, certainly among the most beautiful things she had ever seen, whether in nature or man-made.

"I love him," Miranda whispered, surprising herself with the revelation. It seemed to strike her at the very moment she said it; she had fallen in love with this man who, even in a few short days' time, had made her feel special, needed. For the very first time. "I think I have since the first time I saw him, at Springwater."

She bit down on her lower lip. "You needn't worry, though, because he still cares for you. I reckon he always will." She sighed. "I've got to get back now. The baby might wake up, or that dratted pot could boil over, and I'd best be thinking about supper, too. I just wanted to — well, I don't rightly know what I wanted to do. Just say a how-do-you-do, I guess."

She stood up straight, lifting her eyes as a breeze blew through the leaves of the trees surrounding Caroline's grave, set them raining down, rustling and bright, in a shower of red and gold, crimson and rust. She was not a fanciful person, and she didn't for a moment think of that occurrence as any sort of blessing, but she felt a certain peace where Caroline was concerned all the same.

The wind picked up as she made her way back to the cabin, and when she got to the yard, she was alarmed to find that the bonfire under the kettle had started to spread into the tall, dry grass and was quickly approaching the house. Miranda had seen the prairies blazing on the journey west, and she felt a rush of fear surge through her like venom from the bite of a giant snake.

Dashing into the house, she snatched up the first blanket she came to and rushed out to battle the fire.

"Landry!" she shrieked, her eyes watering from the smoke by then, her breath coming in coughs and gasps that left her throat raw.

She was barely aware of the approaching riders, or even of Landry, until someone threw her onto the ground and rolled her through the dirt. Only then did she realize that the flames had caught on the hem of her dress.

"Get inside and make sure the baby's all right!" Landry yelled, rising and pulling her up with him in almost the same motion. She could see that part of the fire had reached the door before it had been snuffed out by her efforts. "Then start pumping water!"

She nodded, fairly choking by then, and

rushed in to see that little Isaiah-or-Ezekiel was safe. Indeed, he was cooing and trying to catch his own kicking feet with his fat little hands.

Breathlessly thankful, Miranda murmured a prayer of gratitude, snatched up the water buckets next to the stove, and raced outside again. Landry and the two men helping him — through the smoke Miranda recognized Trey Hargreaves and Doc Parrish — had nearly contained the blaze. When at last the fire was subdued, Landry was so covered in soot that you couldn't even tell he'd been butchering all day.

Grinning, Trey dragged a blackened sleeve across a forehead that nearly matched it. "Next time I come to call," he said, directing his words at Landry, "I'd appreciate it if you'd just offer me coffee and water for my horse."

"Amen," agreed the Doc, just catching his breath. He looked more like a chimney sweep just then than the town doctor. He wasn't much of a talker, Doc Parrish, but he knew his business and he was well-liked at Springwater.

"I'll make the coffee," Miranda said, still hoarse from the smoke, and went inside.

When she came out again, with the handles of three mugs hooked over two fingers of one hand and the coffeepot in the other, the men were seated side by side on the edge of the horse trough, talking seriously. Miranda wasn't an eavesdropper, but when she heard Jacob McCaffrey's name, she stopped to listen and made no effort to hide the fact.

Landry met her gaze, and raised his brimming cup in a gesture that plainly said, "Thank you."

"I was just telling Landry that Mike Houghton's back," Trey said. "Now that the boy's big enough to work for a living, he's come to claim him."

Miranda nearly dropped the coffeepot and splashed her ruined skirts with the grounds. "Toby? But Jacob and June-bug are his family —"

"Be that as it may," the Doc said grimly, "Mike's come to claim him."

Miranda couldn't move for several long moments, she was so stricken by this news. Toby, found by Rachel Hargreaves in an abandoned camp up in the timber about eighteen months before, when she'd first come to Springwater to teach school, had been taken in by the McCaffreys. Jacob, especially, adored the boy, and he was still on the mend from a bad spell with his heart right after the Doc and Savannah got married. He and June-bug had already lost two sons in the war; it might destroy them to give up Toby as well, when they'd come to think of him as their own, and to love him so dearly. Parting would be even worse for young Toby, who had never known a real family before.

"No," she whispered.

"There's nothing anybody can do," the Doc said, to nobody in particular. He was staring off into space. "Toby's still too young to decide for himself, and Houghton *is* his legal father."

Miranda was full of sorrow and fury. "He's no kind of a father!" she spouted. "What kind of man goes off and leaves his own boy to starve in the woods?"

"Miranda," Landry said firmly, but gently, too.

"I've got to go to town," she replied, reaching back, automatically, to untie her apron.

But Landry shook his head. "There'll be preaching on Sunday, like as not. We'll speak to the McCaffreys then."

"But —"

"Miranda."

She went into the house, turning furiously on one heel, but she wasn't happy about it.

Landry Kildare had his share of gall talking to her like that, when he wasn't even a real husband. She was slamming kettles onto the stove and filling them with water from the reservoir when she heard the visitors riding away, heard Landry push open the door and step into the house.

"The boys are staying in town tonight," Landry said. "Toby's their friend."

She didn't turn around, but just went on banging things around. Little Isaiah-or-Ezekiel, far from being frightened, seemed to love the clatter and clang, for he was gurgling away in his basket, happy as a pig in muck.

She stopped. It was a poor choice of images, a pig.

"Miranda, look at me." His voice was quiet, and contained no kind of threat, but she didn't like to disobey him when he spoke to her like that.

She looked. He was black from the fire, and his clothes, first bloodied and now burned and soot-covered, would probably never come clean. "What?"

"There's no point in our going to town ahead of time and adding to the fuss. Jacob and June-bug know we'll come if they need us, and we'll see them day after tomorrow, at the preaching."

It had become rare for Jacob to offer a sermon, though he did on occasion. Landry often took his place, or Tom Bellweather. Since Rachel and Trey Hargreaves' baby had been born, a little boy called Henry, even the keeper of the Brimstone Saloon had been known to get up, on occasion, and hold forth on the sayings of the Good Book.

Tears sprang, unbidden, to her eyes. She dashed at her cheeks with the back of one hand. "I didn't mean for the grass to take fire," she said, because she had to say something to fill the silence, and that was the first thing that came to her mind.

"It wasn't your fault," Landry answered, winding a sooty finger in a loose tendril of her hair. "I'd best go and see to the chores. I'll be in after I've cleaned up."

"I'll go ahead and start supper, then," Miranda said, with a sniffle. She was heartbroken for the McCaffreys and for Toby, that hadn't changed, but Landry was right. It would do no good to go rushing off to town and intrude on a private grief.

On another level, she marveled that he wasn't blaming her for the fire. Her father would have berated her in a loud voice, maybe even beaten her. After all, they might have lost the house, the barn, everything, because of her carelessness and inexperience, but it seemed Landry had already dismissed the whole matter from his mind.

Landry had merely nodded, acknowledging her statement, and left her to her cooking. Only then did she have time to examine the riot of feelings he'd roused in her, just by touching her hair and speaking gently.

When he returned, nearly an hour later, by the loud old clock on one end of the mantel, Miranda had a meal ready to set out, and she nearly dropped the pot of chicken and dumplings at the sight of him. He was merely *clean,* she supposed, with his hair washed and combed through with his fingers, and his clothes all tidy, smelling the way he was supposed to smell, and yet the mere sight of him fairly stopped her heart from beating. If he smiled, she didn't know what she'd do.

He went right ahead and smiled. "Smells good," he said.

Miranda was so dazed that it took her an unlikely amount of time to reason out that he was talking about supper. She nodded, probably looking downright foolish, and set the pot down on the table with a thump. "You start right in. I just want to see if the baby's asleep."

"I'll wait for you," he said, mannerly as a

71

prince in a storybook, standing there behind his chair.

It was useless to protest, Miranda figured, for the man was as stubborn as could be, though she had to admit he was fair-minded. She looked in on little Isaiah-or-Ezekiel, snoozing away in his basket in her bedroom, and returned to the main room.

Landry was still waiting, and patiently. Only when she sat down did he take his chair. As he had done the night before, he led a short, plain prayer of thanks for the food, and then the meal began.

Miranda wondered what was on his mind. He was always gentlemanly, for a man who didn't put on a coat and collar except on Sundays, but he hadn't waited for her to sit down before starting in on last night's supper. She looked at him curiously, figuring that she probably never would understand him, even if she lived to be as old as Granny Johnson, up there on the mountainside.

"I'll be another few days getting those hogs cut up and hung," he said.

Miranda's stomach rolled. She took a sip from her water cup in hopes of settling herself down a little. "What about them — those heads, out there in the cauldron?" she said, in a nigh-unto-normal tone of voice.

Landry was chewing a mouthful of chicken and dumplings. "I reckon you'll be able to put the first batch of meat up in jars tomorrow," he said happily, when he'd swallowed. "I'll make head cheese from the others."

Miranda pushed back her chair, preparatory to rushing for the door. She was no sissy. She'd chopped the heads off chickens before, cleaned and plucked them, too. She'd skinned rabbits for stew and even boiled up a prairie dog once, on the trail from St. Louis, when game had been scarce, but she wasn't going to eat anything that had been scooped out of some critter's skull and that was the end of it.

Landry's eyes were dancing. "It's tasty stuff," he teased.

Much as she cared for him, she could have murdered him just then. He looked as mischievous as one of his boys, sitting there, with one side of his mouth twitching that way, all but wriggling his eyebrows. "I'd rather starve."

"Then I guess you've never been hungry," he answered, and went on eating.

Miranda was finished, but she didn't leave the table. She just sat there, with her hands folded in her lap, waiting. Waiting — for what, she did not know. The place was quiet without the boys, and the very air itself seemed to hum around her ears. The day had been a long and difficult one, and she was tired, but if anything troubled her, it was the vibrant yet ordinary *happiness* of just being there, with Landry.

He tilted his head to one side, taking in the ruined skirts of her dress. "You'll have to cut that up for rags, it looks like," he commented. Apparently, he was in a mood to talk.

The thought horrified Miranda, even though she knew he was right, and very little of the gown would be salvageable. It was the prettiest of her hand-me-downs, having belonged to Rachel Hargreaves, a bright yellow fabric with eyelet at the neckline and mother-of-pearl buttons. She looked down at it sadly and then gave a brief, reluctant nod of agreement.

He looked sympathetic and, at the same time, he seemed a little amused. No doubt, she looked a sight, in her scorched and sooty clothes. The merriment in his eyes made him seem like a scamp, hardly older than his sons. "Don't fret," he said. "We'll get you something twice as pretty when we go to Choteau." He frowned thoughtfully, while spearing yet another dumpling from the kettle in the center of the table. It amazed

Miranda how much the man could eat, and still be made of nothing but muscle and bone. "You'd look real nice in scarlet, I think, or dark blue."

The thought of traveling to Choteau cheered Miranda not a little, but she managed to keep her expression prim and matronly, lest he think she was too eager, or even extravagant. "I don't think proper ladies wear scarlet," she said.

That time, he did laugh, and she was wounded. Didn't he think she was a proper lady? She pushed back her chair and would have fled if he hadn't reached out and caught hold of her wrist when she started past him, on the way to her room.

"Miranda," he said and, just like that, with a simple tug, he pulled her down onto his lap. "I'm sorry," he said. His breath was warm on her face.

She was disturbed by the other complex sensations their proximity wrought in her, too, and none of it helped her mood. "*Yes,*" she hissed, and she could feel her ears throbbing, which meant they were probably red as a rooster's comb, "I made a mistake. I trusted a man I shouldn't have trusted. But that doesn't mean I'm not a decent woman, Landry Kildare!"

He was still smiling, damn him, but the

light in his eyes was tender. He laid the tip of one index finger against her mouth to silence her. "Hush," he said. "I laughed because, all of the sudden, I had a picture of you in my mind, stirring that pot out in the dooryard today, twisted halfway to Texas to keep from looking in and seeing hog eyeballs looking back at you."

His thighs were hard as tamarack, and so was his chest. His arms, though loosely clasped, nonetheless encircled her. She could barely think. "Maybe you should let me up," she said lamely.

He sighed. "I know for sure that I should," he agreed, "but damn if I can make myself do it. We'll take the stage to Choteau in a week, Miranda. We can stay in a hotel and take all our meals in restaurants, just like we were on a honeymoon. Do you think you'll be ready by then — to share my bed, I mean?"

She wanted to say she was ready *now,* but that would only have made him think twice about counting her a lady. Miranda knew almost nothing about the relations between a husband and wife, despite the fact that she'd already borne a child, but she understood that it wasn't proper to be too eager, even when the man was your honest-to-God, by-the-Good-Book husband. "I — I guess," she answered miserably. "As long as you don't smell like pigs."

He laughed again, actually threw back his head and shouted with it, but that time, she didn't take offense. Heaven only knew how long he would have held her there, perched on his lap and feeling all her vital organs melt, one by one, into a hot puddle deep inside her, if little Isaiah-or-Ezekiel hadn't let out a wail when he did.

Landry put his hands on Miranda's waist and lifted her to her feet, and she made for the bedroom, lickety-split. When she returned, after nursing the baby and holding him until he went back to sleep, she was surprised to find Landry at the sink, drying the last of the supper dishes.

She had never seen a man do that, and the sight made her mouth fall open. She closed it right away, but not quickly enough to keep Landry from seeing how startled she was.

He chuckled and shook his head. "There's plenty of hot water in the reservoir," he said. "If you'd like to take a bath, I mean."

Miranda swallowed. Either he was insulting her again, or he was trying to drive her crazy. It was hard to tell which one. She might have broke right down and cried with confusion, if she hadn't had just a shred of pride left. "Kind of you to offer," she said, though she didn't know whether that was the truth or not.

"I'll carry the tub into the spare room for you," he said, "or you can bathe out here, in front of the fire."

"Where will you be all this time?" she wanted to know. She might have been a lot of things, but immodest wasn't one of them.

His face cracked into a grin, but he made a creditable effort at looking serious. "In my room," he said. "I like to read a little while before I turn down the lights."

Miranda closed her eyes for an instant. She could imagine him in that room, in that big, Landry-scented bed, only too well. And after the trip to Choteau, she'd be sharing it with him, unless he found her wanting in some way. "All right, then," she said, agreeing to the bath and a whole lot more, if you wanted to know the plain truth.

Fortunately, Landry didn't pursue the matter. He just brought the tub in from one of the sheds, set it in front of the hearth, and began filling it with water. It was still steaming when he set out a towel and a bar of soap and left her to herself. She was out of her clothes and into that bath quicker than quick, and sunk right down to her chin. It was blissful, and she let out a long breath in sheer appreciation, but soon enough she got bored, idling in the middle of what served as a parlor, wearing nothing but soap suds and a washtub, and finished up her bath. Climbing out, she wrapped herself in Landry's towel — she hadn't thought to fetch a nightgown — and tiptoed toward her room.

As she passed, the line of light underneath his door faded to darkness.

4

Needless to say, Miranda was surprised to run into the big boar the next morning, when she carried out a bucketful of scraps to feed the yearling pigs. She'd thought he was in the jars and crocks she'd been sealing with hot wax since just after breakfast or, at the very least, hanging in the smokehouse along with several of his lady friends.

Instead, he was on the loose, facing Miranda on the path, snorting ominously and pawing at the ground with one front hoof, just like a bull. In fact, he looked big as a bull to Miranda at that moment. He was as dangerous as he was ugly, a quarter ton of sorry pork, with a mean spirit and a made-up mind.

Shakily, Miranda tossed the scraps to the ground, pail and all. There were barely four feet between her and the boar by then, and though he snuffled the offering of stale bread, potato peelings, eggshells, coffee grounds, and the like, it didn't hold his interest long. He raised that massive head again right away and fixed his little eyes on her.

"L-Landry," she called, in an almost musical tone, as though being real polite would somehow keep the pig from charging and tearing her apart with razor-sharp teeth.

"Don't move," Landry advised, from a few feet behind her. She was so relieved at his presence that she nearly fainted dead away, but in the next instant, the boar charged, with a horrifying, squeal-like bellow. The whole universe seemed to slow down; Miranda heard a rifle being cocked, then the loud report of a gunshot. The beast fell, inches shy of where she stood, its head a bloody pulp, already drawing flies.

Miranda got messages from a hundred parts of herself, body and soul, and all in the space of a heartbeat. Someone cowering in a rear corner of her brain was screaming in shrill terror, and it was only by the grace of God and good muscle tone that she held on to the contents of her bladder. Her stomach bounced between her throat and her hip bones, unsure where to settle.

She stood frozen for what seemed a long time, trying to put herself back together. She watched like a detached spectator as

Landry passed her, laid his rifle on the ground, and crouched down to inspect the dead boar. She began to weep, but silently, for she couldn't seem to force out a sound — not a sob, a shriek, or even a hiccough.

Landry rose to his full height again, rifle in hand once more, shaking his head and looking sadly down at the animal who had just attacked his wife. "That," he said, "was a perfectly good hog."

The words loosed Miranda's locked knees, and she turned, one hand pressed to her mouth, and fled into the cabin. All the rest of the day, while she preserved what seemed like an endless supply of pig meat, following the instructions in an old cookery book that had, of course, belonged to Caroline, she relived the whole episode, from the first fearsome comprehension that the boar meant to rip her apart where she stood, to the gunshot, to Landry's words.

That was a perfectly good hog.

Landry gazed ruefully down at the dead boar and wondered how the hell the miserable critter had gotten out of the holding pen. He'd planned to keep the animal for a long while, and use him for breeding, but now he wasn't good for a whole lot more than ham and bacon. God knew, there'd be no head cheese from this one.

He sighed. He still had yearlings, and a couple of them were boars. There were three young sows, too, which meant he'd have another crop of piglets in the spring. No sense in stewing over what couldn't be helped; he was still in the hog business, after all.

He glanced toward the house, where Miranda had fled just moments before. Only then did he allow himself to think of what could have happened to her, what *would* have happened, if he hadn't seen her trying to face down that evil-natured pig. His stomach pitched, and he thought for a moment that he'd be sick, right there in the barnyard. However long he lived, he didn't reckon he'd ever forget looking down the barrel of that rifle, so scared that his heart was jammed into his throat fit to cut off his wind, and pulling the trigger.

He thought about going into the house and trying to soothe Miranda, maybe even taking her into his arms, the way he would have done with Caroline, but he felt strangely tongue-tied, and he had more than a day's work yet to do and a lot less time to do it. Besides, he smelled like pig.

With another sigh, he made for the barn, left the rifle leaning against an outside wall, and went in to hitch up Nicodemus, the strongest of his two plow horses. Then, using about equal portions of muscle and sweat, he and the horse dragged the boar behind one of the sheds, where Landry, cursing every now and again, skinned the hog, and cleaned it.

He worked through the afternoon and well into the evening; only when he saw lamplight coming from the cabin windows did he realize it was dark. Resigned, exasperated, and hurting in every joint and sinew, he went down to the creek with a bar of soap and the clean clothes Miranda had at some point left for him by the smokehouse door, and gave himself a scrubbing in water cold enough to set his teeth to chattering.

When he got inside the house, every inch of him covered in goosebumps, hungry as a bear in April, there was no sign of supper, and Miranda was seated at the table, bent over what looked like a reading primer. Little One-or-the-other was in the basket, waving and kicking and making baby sounds for all he was worth.

Miranda had been so engrossed in the shabby little book that Landry's entrance must have startled her, for she jumped half out of her skin when he shut the door. Then, almost guiltily, she slammed the volume shut and put it on her lap. Her cheeks were glowing with either embarrassment or indignation, maybe even both, and her eyes had a snap in them.

Landry felt a muscle bunch in his jaw. He'd be damned if he understood women — he'd saved that milk-and-honey hide of hers, and killed the best pig he'd ever owned in the process, and despite all that, she was in a pet. He lowered the door latch with a *thump* meant to show that he wasn't going to put up with any nonsense.

"I'm hungry," he said, hanging up his hat. "What's for supper?"

Her gaze cut toward the warming oven above the stove. "Pig," she said.

He wanted to laugh, all of the sudden, but he couldn't figure why. He went to the stove, opened the door on the warming oven, and peered in to see a plate heaped with shredded pork, boiled to a thought-provoking shade of gray. Quick as that, his mirth dissipated. He was so irritated that he forgot to use a pot holder when he reached in to retrieve the plate and burned his fingers good.

He was cursing under his breath as he wadded up a flour-sack dish towel, got the plate out, and dumped everything on it into the scrap bucket. Then he went to the pantry to fetch some hard, dry bread and a hunk of even drier, harder cheese to appease his growling stomach.

Miranda narrowed her eyes at him, but she didn't say a single, solitary word. She just sat there, hiding that reading primer, or whatever it was, and glaring at him, like she was glad — *glad* he'd burned himself and was now reduced to eating victuals better suited to a flock of chickens than a full-grown man who'd just put in sixteen hours of dirty, back-breaking work.

He slapped the bleak meal he'd scrounged from the pantry onto a blue spatterware plate, carried it to the table, and set it down with a crash before dropping into his chair. He had been unjustly used and he wanted her to know it.

She didn't back down an inch.

The standoff continued until Landry had choked down enough food to ease his stomach pangs; after that, he couldn't force another bite past his lips. "What's in the book?" he snapped, because something had to be said or he was going to go crazy, and everything else he could think of was down-right inflammatory.

She blushed; even in the dim light, he could see that. Her jaw jutted out slightly, though just for a moment, then she lowered her eyes and her shoulders went slack. He'd won, after a fashion, but he didn't feel especially good about it. He didn't even feel vindicated.

"You've got to promise not to make fun of me if I tell," she said, after a long time. He nodded his agreement, then she laid the book on the table between them, still avoiding his gaze.

It was a tattered, falling-apart copy of McGuffy's Reader, which didn't surprise him, of course, because he'd thought he recognized it. They were both silent. Miranda chewed on her lower lip, and Landry simply waited. He wished that he hadn't challenged her, but there was no going back now.

"I can read," she protested. "Don't you go thinking I can't."

He simply watched her. There were a lot of people who struggled with the printed word; it came as no particular surprise that she might be one of them.

"It's just that it's — hard for me." Her eyes filled with tears of humiliation and of desperate dignity. "I'm bound to get real good at it, though," she added, with determination.

He reached across the table, laid a hand over hers. "I'm sorry, Miranda," he said.

She sniffled and jerked her hand back. "Don't you dare feel pity for me, Landry Kildare!" she cried, and the baby, alarmed, began to fuss.

Perhaps from old habit, Landry got to the basket before she did, picked up the infant, and held him the same way he'd held Jamie and Marcus, when they were little. "I didn't say I felt sorry for you," he told Miranda, patting the baby's small, heaving back with one hand. "All I meant was, I wanted things to be all right between us again. That's all."

She deflated a little, and there was something of softness, something of incredulity in her eyes as she watched him with her son. What was it, he wondered, that made women believe they were the only ones capable of holding a baby? It wasn't like the little critters weighed anything at all.

Miranda lifted the corner of her apron and dried her eyes with it. She was just standing there, sniffling and looking mournful, and for once, it seemed she had nothing to say.

"Miranda, in the name of God, what is it?" Landry asked tightly. The baby fretted; he bounced him a little. Settled him right down.

For a moment there, it looked like she was going to come straight out and tell him, but in the end, she just walked over, took the baby from him, and disappeared into her bedroom. She came back only to fetch the basket, by which time Landry was back in the pantry, searching for something else to eat.

Despite his exhaustion, he read far into the night, unable to settle his mind, and five minutes after he'd turned down the wick on his bedside lamp, Miranda started screaming fit to start up the resurrection of the saints ahead of schedule. By the time Landry pounded through her door, wearing nothing but his long johns, the baby was howling too.

Frankly, Landry had expected a band of renegade Indians or a bobcat, at the very least, but all he found was Miranda sitting up in bed, sucking in air in great, panicked gasps, and the baby yelling in sympathy.

He jiggled the basket, somewhat hurriedly, on his way to Miranda. "There now, little fella," he said, wishing the kid had a manageable name, "it'll be all right." He had barely sat down on the edge of the spare room bed — he hadn't realized it was so narrow and so hard — when Miranda flung both arms around his neck and clung to him like a swimmer about to go under. He hesitated only a fraction of a moment before enfolding her in a cautious embrace of his own.

"That pig," she sputtered into the curve between his neck and shoulder, "that awful pig was after me —"

"Shhh," he said, and brushed his lips across her temple. It wasn't really a kiss, he told himself. "It was just a dream. Nothing's going to hurt you." He was struck by the emphasis he'd put on that assurance — the desire to protect Miranda from anything and anyone meaning her harm was almost overwhelming. Even there, in what had always been Caroline's sanctuary, he found he couldn't quite remember his first wife's face. Her image was fading from his mind, like thin ink on an old letter.

It shamed him, this forgetting of a woman he'd sworn to remember unto death and beyond, and yet he couldn't seem to put Miranda from him. She was so warm, so soft, so sweet. And she was weeping into his shoulder.

"Shhh," he said again, and smoothed her tangle of silky hair with one hand. The baby, at least, was settling down a little, just hiccoughing now and again.

"B-because of me," Miranda wailed, "a pig is d-dead!"

Landry might have smiled, under other

circumstances, but this, of course, was not the time. Besides, he was too stricken by the discovery that he couldn't call Caroline to mind the way he always had before. He held Miranda away so he could look into her face. It was awash in moonlight and tears, and unbelievably beautiful.

"Hush," he said, with a sort of tender sternness. "There'll be other boars."

She snuffled, her small shoulders moving in the effort to calm herself. Her eyes sought Landry in the gloom, still opaque with fear and bright as buttons. "I-I was so scared," she confessed, and he knew she wasn't talking about the dream, now, but about the actual confrontation with that devil's whelp of a hog. "I've heard so many stories —"

Landry kissed her forehead; he wasn't sure why. It was a light kiss, a kiss in passing, but it left him troubled all the same, first because he did it in the place that had been Caroline's refuge, and second because it only left him wanting more. So much more.

"You've got to let that go," he counseled, and he wondered if he was talking to himself in some ways as well as to Miranda. "There's nothing to be gained by going over what happened today, either waking or sleeping. The important thing is, you're alive." Dear God, wasn't she, though?

Holding her like that made Landry feel things he didn't remember feeling before, ever. Not even with Caroline, who was the only other woman he'd ever been intimate with.

"He'll come back — he'll be right there in my head, soon as I close my eyes —"

"No," Landry said. "I won't let that happen." With that, he lay down beside her on that skinny bed, he in his underwear, she in her nightdress, and kept his arms wrapped around her. "Go to sleep now, Miranda," he said, though he didn't figure he'd close his own eyes all night. "We'll have to be up early to get the chores done before it's time to leave for the preaching."

She allowed him to hold her, even settled comfortably into his arms. It was torture for him, though; he was as engorged as a stallion mounting a mare, but with no honorable way to relieve the agony. He wondered what she'd do if he made love to her, slowly and tenderly, but he made no move to find out. He'd given his word, after all, and he meant to keep it, whatever the cost to his own sanity.

Miranda awakened just before dawn and saw Landry through her lashes, sitting on the edge of the bed with his head in his hands. It was a moment or two before she remembered her nightmare, and how he had come to her, and held her, and lay down beside her just so she'd feel safe. She'd known he wanted her; she'd felt that, what with the two of them lying so close together and all, and she would not have refused him. All the same, he hadn't made her his real wife, perhaps because this room was a reminder of Caroline.

She put a hand out, touched his warm, solid back. He was wearing long johns, and he managed to make even those look good. "It's all right," she said, very softly. She didn't know what made her choose those particular words; maybe it was just that he'd used them to reassure her the night before, after that terrible dream.

He didn't answer, not directly, at any rate. From his words, you'd have thought she hadn't said anything at all. "I'll get the stove going," he said. "You stay in bed a little while."

She didn't want to let him go. "Landry," she said softly.

The muscles in his back hardened beneath her hand. Maybe he thought she was about to try and seduce him, and had set himself to resist. "In a quarter of an hour or so, you might get up and start breakfast. I'll see to the chores and get the buckboard ready for the drive to Springwater."

They were going to the preaching, she recalled, with a little swell of joy. She had forgotten that. She bit her lower lip to keep from leaning forward and kissing the curve of his shoulder. "Landry," she repeated, with a sort of gentle insistence.

He turned his head, at long last, and looked down into her eyes.

She cupped his cheek with her hand, felt the rough stubble of a new beard, the strong bones of his face. "Thank you."

He looked puzzled.

"For shooting a perfectly good hog yesterday, to save me. For coming in here when I had a nightmare, and for staying so I could sleep without being afraid. The McCaffreys have been good to me and little Isaiah-or-Ezekiel, and so have the other folks at Springwater, but nobody's ever, well, looked after me the way you do."

"Miranda?" There was a light in his eyes again, and the faintest hint of a smile twitched at the corner of his mouth.

"What?"

"Give that baby one name or the other. Sometime soon, he's going to start wondering who the heck he is."

She smiled, and it was hard not to put her

arms around him again, and kiss him on that square chin of his, or that wonderful mouth. "I reckon you're right," she said. "I had a mind to get him named proper by now, but more's happened to me in the last few days than in my whole life put together, it seems like. I haven't had time to think which I ought to call him."

He touched the tip of her nose with a work-callused index finger, and she thought, out of the blue, of that carving he'd made for Caroline's grave. It turned the moment sober again, the remembrance of that exquisite marker. It was a monument to an even more exquisite love, Miranda knew, and if she wanted to get her heart broken right in two, all she needed to do was forget that.

Landry had been about to say something, but now he frowned slightly. "What are you thinking?"

She couldn't tell him, not then. Nor did she want him to leave her just yet, even though she had more of a sense than ever that she had no right to this man. He still belonged to Caroline, a loving and faithful husband in death as well as life.

"I'd like you to help me," she said. "Think up a proper name for the baby, I mean. What would you call him if he was yours?"

95

"He is mine," Landry said, flooding her heart with light just like that. "I reckon of the two names — both of them are good, right out of the Old Testament and all — I favor Isaiah. I like the sound of it, and Isaiah's is the book I like best."

Miranda felt a mixture of sadness and joy — it was, for those few moments, as though she and Landry truly had conceived this baby together. As though Landry were her own, and not Caroline's. "All right, then," she agreed, "it's Isaiah, then."

He smiled. "Isaiah it is," he said. Then he stood to leave the room. "I'd better get to those chores of mine."

"I'll have breakfast made when you come in," she said. It felt good, having someone to say simple, homey things like that to, Caroline or no Caroline.

"You'll need to gather the eggs first," he told her. "I'll milk the cow."

She nodded, and then he was gone. She heard him enter his room, leave it again after a few minutes, heard the stove lids clattering as he built up the fire.

Miranda fed Isaiah — it sounded big on such a little baby, that lofty name, but she knew her son would grow into it in time — bathed and changed him, and carried him with her in the improvised sling while she fetched the eggs. She was at the stove, fixing bacon, of course, and eggs, when Landry came in, wearing his work clothes and carrying a bucket of fresh milk.

He set the bucket on the small worktable next to the stove, and Miranda was painfully aware of him, even though she tried not to let it show. Every time he got close to her, it seemed, she started melting inside, like a honeycomb abandoned to the summer sun.

"You might want to put that boy on cow's milk pretty soon," he said.

Miranda felt a blush climb her neck, and she was glad to have the bacon and eggs to fool around with. She didn't have to ask why Landry had suggested weaning the baby, because she knew it was one of two reasons: either he didn't want to take an infant along to Choteau on their honeymoon trip, or he wanted her breasts for purposes of his own. Both ideas filled her with heat.

"Miranda?"

She had to answer, had to say something. "Breakfast is ready," she told him, and filled a plate for him from the pans on the stove. She herself had no appetite, though she might be ready to eat after the preaching. She'd pack a basket for picnicking under the trees next to the Springwater station, just the way the other wives did.

He wasn't going to be put off that easily. "Miranda," he said again, and more firmly this time.

She met his gaze. She loved that baby, loved him more than her life, but nursing him was hard, when she had so many other things to do, and there could be no arguing that he was a sturdy little mite, off to a real good start in life. And, even though it would be a wrench to leave Isaiah behind with June-bug or maybe Rachel or Savannah for a few days, she wanted that time with Landry more than a mortal being had the right to want anything. "He'll need a bottle," she said.

Landry grinned. "That's easy," he replied. He disappeared into the pantry and, after the sound of much rummaging, came out with a baby bottle in each hand. "They just need washing up. Jamie and Marcus used them when they were little."

Miranda nodded and flushed again. "Sit down and eat your breakfast, Landry Kildare," she said, feeling like a real wife, "before it gets cold."

He sat. "Aren't you going to eat?"

She shook her head. "I'm not ready to face pig meat just yet," she admitted frankly.

Landry chuckled. "Well, you'd better

learn to like it, Mrs. Kildare, because you've married a hog farmer."

"You've got horses, and a few cattle, too," Miranda argued, but good-naturedly, pouring coffee for herself. "I'd rather think of you as a rancher."

He gestured toward her unoccupied place at the table, just as good-naturedly. "Get yourself a plate," he persisted. "I won't have the town of Springwater saying Landry Kildare has a puny wife."

She still wasn't hungry, but she managed to put away half an egg and some toasted bread, just because she was so pleased at Landry's teasing attentions. Why, he talked to her the same way Trey talked to Rachel, and the Doc talked to Savannah. If only he could really make room for her, in that stubborn, loyal heart of his, alongside the hollow place Caroline had left behind.

The dooryard of the Springwater station seemed crowded with buggies and wagons, tethered mules, and horses. Some of the men, Tom Bellweather, Trey Hargreaves, and the Doc, were out front, under the front slant of the roof, handsome in their best clothes. Their expressions were serious, though, and Miranda knew they were talking about Mike Houghton's return, and the effect his claim on Toby might have on the McCaffreys.

Miranda was more than anxious to speak with Jacob and June-bug, and see with her own eyes that they were holding up under the strain, but she had Isaiah in her arms and thus waited until Landry had braked the buckboard, secured the reins, and then jumped down and came around the side to help her to the ground.

While Landry tarried outside with the other men, Miranda hurried inside. As was usual for a Sunday morning, the tables had been moved to one side of the large main room of the station, thus making room for the benches to be lined up before the hearth, pew-style. Jacob usually stood in front of the fireplace when he was preaching, a habit he'd acquired, he was fond of saying, over the course of a dozen harsh territorial winters.

There was no sign of him now, although June-bug was standing over by the stove, stirring something, and Rachel and Savannah were close by, doing little keep-busy tasks so they'd have an excuse to hover. Miranda wanted to be a member of that group as much as she wanted anything except Landry's love, but this was no time to be thinking about what she wanted, so she put it out of her mind.

Seeing her and the baby June-bug came forward and gently tucked back the blanket. "Would you look at him?" she said, smiling a wan ghost of a smile. "I swear he's grown just since you and Landry got hitched the other day."

Savannah stepped forward. "Could I hold him, Miranda?" she asked softly.

It was no secret how much the Parrishes wanted a baby, and everybody knew they hadn't gotten one started yet, too. That was the way of a small place like Springwater; there weren't many secrets. Miranda smiled and handed Isaiah over to the other woman. Then she put her arms around June-bug and hugged her tight.

June-bug, usually so spry and energetic, felt fragile in her arms, as though something had broken down inside her and she just couldn't get it mended. She clung to Miranda for a long moment, then thrust herself away, with a sniffle and an attempt at a laugh. "Here I am, on the Lord's day, actin' like I don't have a whit of faith," she said.

Rachel, still plump from the birth of her own baby, was peering into the basket where her little Henry slept, looking like an angel. She fussed with the blankets. "Where is

Jacob?" she asked of June-bug, in a tone so careful that Miranda knew she'd been waiting for a good time to put forward the question.

"He took a walk down to the springs, him and Toby both," June-bug answered, and that faraway, misty look was back in her eyes. It crushed Miranda's heart to see this woman who had been so kind to her feeling so unhappy, and being so brave in the face of it. The McCaffreys had suffered enough, by her reckoning, losing not one but both their own boys on the same battlefield. "Toby's been talkin' about runnin' away, lightin' out for Mexico or some such nonsense. Jacob's tryin' to make him see reason and stay with his daddy, if that's what it comes down to, but that boy is hard-headed and he's got ideas of his own."

Toby was indeed hard-headed, but he was a good boy, and he'd make a fine man one day, thanks to the McCaffreys. Provided Mike Houghton didn't turn him into a robber or a drunk, anyhow. He ran with bad companions, Houghton did; everybody knew that.

"He'll be all right," Rachel said, with spirit, but she looked worried all the same. She too had a special interest in Toby, having found him in the woods the way she had and brought him home to Springwater, where she'd been his teacher up until baby Henry came into the world. "He's one of us. He belongs here."

At that, all the women looked at each other, as if seeking assurance that what Rachel said was true. All of them except Savannah, that is, who was gazing down at little Isaiah with her heart shining in her eyes.

5

Miranda's first sight of Jacob, when he entered the station with a red-eyed, rebellious-looking Toby in tow, left her heart as crackly as an old china plate. He was painfully thin and seemed no more substantial than if he'd had hay for stuffing, like some wind-whipped scarecrow, instead of muscle and bone and vitals. His dark eyes, always so solemn and so kindly, seemed to have sunk deep into his head. Only the determined set of his jaw gave cause for hope — the fight had not gone out of him entirely, then. She was relieved to know that much.

"Hello, Toby," Miranda said quietly, and crossed the room to lay a hand on the boy's thin shoulder. During her time at Springwater station, she'd come to know Toby and to respect him for his diligence and his loyalty to the McCaffreys. He'd be a big man one day, but at twelve, nearly thirteen, he was still more sapling than tree.

His blue eyes locked with Miranda's, full of angry misery, and in that moment she wanted to crush him to her and hold him tightly until Mike Houghton gave up and went away. That would have done no good, of course, even if Toby would have stood still for it. "I don't want to go," he said.

Miranda pressed her lips together and looked up at Jacob. His face echoed the sorrow she'd seen in Toby's. Again, it came to her that this trial might be the one that finally broke an otherwise unbreakable man.

"Where is Mr. Houghton now?" she asked of Jacob, her hand still resting on Toby's shoulder. He would tolerate little in the way of coddling, she knew, but he permitted her that much.

Jacob's voice was a hollow boom, but there was some of the old thunder in it, faint as it was, like the rumble of a storm a-borning on the far horizon. "He's camped outside of town. Said he'd be by for the preachin' this mornin'."

Miranda's hackles rose at that; there was a thing or two she wanted to say to Toby's so-called father, but she knew it would be a waste of breath. Some people were just so mean and greedy that nothing would shame them into behaving like they should. She'd had a father like that herself; only reason he'd kept her around after her ma died was so he'd have somebody to do the cooking and the wash. The sad truth was, Houghton was sure to tire of Toby at some point and turn him out, just as her pa had done, only he'd likely do it someplace far from Springwater and the McCaffreys. With all these thoughts showing plain in her eyes, she was sure, she ruffled the boy's fair hair, felt him tremble under her hand.

Folks began to arrive in earnest after that, and soon everyone had taken their places on the benches facing the hearth in the main room of the station. Jacob, unable to preach for some time, stood shaky but proud before his small congregation, and offered up a ringing prayer to get things started. The day being warm and fair for October, the door stood open, and when Mike Houghton stepped over the threshold, he seemed to bring a spine-stinging winter wind right along with him.

Everyone turned in mid-hymn, having sensed his presence, and one by one the various voices fell away, until there was nothing left of sound but for the slow, insolent clapping of Houghton's beefy hands.

He was a brute, brawny as a stagecoach mule, fairly filling that doorway, and Miranda suspected folks would hardly have been more taken aback to see the devil himself standing there. He wore a dirty leather vest over a colorless shirt, threadbare trousers with that, and scuffed boots, run down at the heel and in sore need of mending. His hat looked like he'd left it in the road for a month or two.

"Come in," Jacob greeted him, as he would have done any other man, "and join us in worshiping the Lord."

Houghton ambled inside, without bothering to remove his hat, and out of the corner of her eye, Miranda saw Landry's jawline tighten as he watched the other man's entrance. For all that her husband was in most respects a stranger to her, she knew this was not a good sign.

"Polecat!" somebody cried out, and Miranda realized it was Granny Johnson who'd spoken up. She might have smiled if the situation hadn't been so delicate. The old woman was likely to say whatever came to her mind, and wouldn't spare the horses. Saint Paul himself probably couldn't have talked her into taking back what she'd said, so no one made the effort.

"Now, that ain't no kind of Christian welcome," Mike Houghton said, taking off his hat at last, revealing a head of thinning, oily hair and a freckled pate. Clutching the hat to his chest in a mocking show of respect for everyone present, he took in the assemblage arrayed on either side of the narrow aisle between the rows of benches.

Miranda sought Toby with her eyes — he'd been seated next to June-bug the last time she'd seen him, with Marcus and Jamie at his other side, looking as fiercely defiant as their young friend — but there was no sign of him now. Her stepsons, she noted, with a sense of slow but heightening alarm, were gone, too. Another sidelong glance at her husband revealed that he'd noticed the absence as well, whether or not he'd felt called upon to comment.

Jacob, meanwhile, left his post in front of the fireplace and came forward to meet Houghton. "Sit down, brother, and join us in raising our prayers and songs of praise. Your business here will wait."

"I came to get my boy." Houghton looked around, as though Jacob hadn't spoken at all. "Where's he got to?" He returned his gaze to the man before him. "If you've hid him someplace. Preacher, you'd best tell me where, so I don't have to do anything to upset these good folks."

At this, moving almost as one, Landry, Tom Bellweather, Trey Hargreaves, Scully Wainwright, and Doc Parrish all left their various places in the congregation, found their way to the front of the room, and aligned themselves behind Jacob. Although she feared violence — she'd never seen anything good come of it, not one time — Miranda was prouder than ever, in that moment, that Landry was her husband. Even if he was so in the legal respect only.

Houghton paused and rubbed his chin with one hand, assuming an injured expression, as though he'd come in expecting hospitality and been ill-used instead. "I just want my boy," he said. He sounded pitiful that time, and if she hadn't known the true facts, Miranda might actually have felt sorry for him.

Jacob searched the room with genuine concern, clearly looking for Toby, and June-bug, hands clenched tightly in her lap, turned from her customary seat on the bench up front and did the same. A murmur arose from the congregation as other people began to realize that young Houghton really *had* vanished, and only the five men aligned behind Jacob remained as they were, watchful and ready to fight, be it the Sabbath Day or not.

"He was here when I started the prayer," Jacob said quietly. He met Houghton's gaze and did not flinch or look away. "We'll find him soon as the service is over."

For a long time, he and Houghton just stood there, staring at each other, like an archangel and a demon come face-to-face over the same broken and straying soul, both of them set to lay claim. Then, remarkably, Toby's long-absent father sat himself down, right up front. Sue Bellweather moved over to make room for him, but stiffly. The brim of her Sunday bonnet hid her face, but Miranda didn't need to see to know the other woman's countenance was not one of welcome.

The hymn went unsung, and Jacob started right in on the preaching, but folks were mostly interested in what Mike Houghton might do, so nobody paid much attention. Landry and the others remained where they were, throughout the whole remainder of the sermon — a well-planned and pointed message about the love between Abraham and Isaac.

Miranda kept looking for her mischievous stepsons, but they were just as gone as Toby, and she knew, as Landry surely did, that Jamie and Marcus had spirited the Houghton boy away. Heaven only knew where they might have hidden him; they were as footloose as prairie savages, those boys — when they weren't in church, at school, or directly under Landry's eye — and they knew the terrain for literally miles around. They could probably hide out until the first snow, maybe longer, and stay unfound as long as they considered necessary.

At one and the same time, Miranda feared for their safety and wished them Godspeed. They might be going about it all wrong, but their motives couldn't be faulted — they were trying to protect their friend. Watching Landry's stiff face, she wondered what he was thinking, if indeed he might not know precisely where his sons — and Toby — had gone.

"I'll have the law down on the whole lot of you," Houghton threatened, rising to his feet. He was sweating under the arms and blotted his beaded forehead on the sleeve of his shirt. He swayed, stabbing a fat index finger in Jacob's direction, and Miranda realized he was drunk. "I want my boy, and I want him now. You bring him on out here, Preacher, or you'll be sorry."

Jacob hardly seemed intimidated, though he was a much older man than Houghton, and at a physical disadvantage, too, despite his own significant size, because of his recent illness. His gaunt face was flushed, and his eyes seemed to blaze with righteous fury, and it seemed to Miranda that he stood taller in those moments than he had in a long while. "Sit yourself down, brother," he told Houghton, and when he seemed a bit unsteady on his feet, and Trey and Landry stepped forward to grasp his elbows in an offer of support, he shrugged them off. "I believe we ought to sing another hymn before we leave off worshipin'."

Houghton hesitated, cast an assessing glance around the room, perhaps to see if he had any supporters in the crowd, and then, amazingly, sank back to his bench.

Miranda thought she'd never heard a congregation sing with such spirit before, but then, she'd had few enough opportunities to attend church in the years since her mother's passing. Her father was not a religious man.

Finally, however, the service was truly over, and the women of the community gathered around June-bug, patting and smiling and embracing Mrs. McCaffrey and then one another, as women will do in times of difficulty. They included Miranda in their circle as though she had always been one of them, and that warmed her through and through. Rachel even went so far as to remark that marriage seemed to agree with Miranda, as well as with Landry, and June-bug, though fitful and distracted, allowed as how she had not seen Landry look so hearty in all the time she'd known him.

Mike Houghton, meanwhile, had been shepherded outside by the men, and although the occasional raised voice pierced the chinked log walls of the station, Jacob's and Houghton's being the most easily recognized, the brawl Miranda had half-expected did not come.

In time, Landry came in to collect her and baby Isaiah. After taking the infant from the large basket he'd shared with Rachel and Trey's Henry, Miranda kissed June-bug on the cheek and made her promise that she'd send word if she had a need of company. Only when she was seated in the wagon beside Landry, and well away from the church, did Miranda speak of the three missing boys.

"Do you know where they are?" she asked.

Landry considered. "They could be any one of a thousand places," he said, with a sigh. "I've let them run wild since Caroline passed on, and this is what comes of it."

On impulse, Miranda linked her arm loosely through his. True, he had spoken of Caroline, but that was to be expected, given that he'd been married to the woman and fathered two children by her. There was a tense moment, but Landry did not pull away. "But Toby is with them?" Miranda asked.

"I'm sure of it," Landry said, with a crisp nod. "I suppose they figure if they just stay gone long enough, Houghton will give up and move on."

"Will he?"

Landry heaved a sigh, then shook his head. "I don't reckon so," he said. "He's got some use in mind for the boy — probably to keep track of the horses while he and his friends hold up banks and stagecoaches."

Miranda shivered, held her baby son close against her chest, even though he was well protected from the cold, being bundled in a woolen blanket Landry had searched out before they left the ranch for the preaching. "Toby could be shot," she protested, "or arrested and hanged."

"Houghton figures he's expendable, I expect."

"Ex— ?"

Landry's mouth crooked upwards at one side, but his eyes were kind. "Expendable. Something — or somebody — a person can get by without."

Miranda ran her teeth over her lower lip once, weighing the word and its definition.

"My pa felt the same way about me," she said. *And so does my husband,* she added to herself. There was no bid for sympathy in her tone when she spoke aloud; what she meant was, she understood some of what Toby must feel. "What was your family like, Landry? The home-folks, I mean?"

He grinned at some private memory, urged the team to a slightly faster pace. The hills made a spectacle of brilliant color in the distance, and the air was sharp with the approach of winter. "My pa was a good man," Landry replied. "He had a fair-sized farm, back in Missouri. Caroline's family leased the land next to ours. I had two younger sisters and an older brother — my brother, Jack, died in the war, and one of my sisters, Mary Elizabeth, passed on, too, of a fever. My other sister, Polly, is a school-marm, like Rachel was."

There were more questions Miranda wanted to ask, flocks of them, but she didn't want to pry. "Your mother?"

"She died when I was little. Pa remarried her first cousin, Ruth. She had Mary Elizabeth and Polly. She still lives on the home place, though Pa died five years ago, around the time we lost Caroline."

Miranda held her tongue. There was ever so much she wanted to know about Caroline, but she wasn't going to ask. She *wasn't.*

He didn't volunteer anything more, either. Naturally, his mind was on the whereabouts of his sons, and young Toby, of course. "I'll see you and the baby home safe," he said, "and go out looking for those three little hooligans. I just hope I find them before they get themselves caught in an early snowstorm or come across some slat-ribbed cougar."

She hadn't allowed herself to think as far as wild animals and uncertain weather, not to mention the many other dangers the wilderness had to offer. Now, she cast a nervous glance at the sky. It was still a heart-piercing blue, that sky, with no clouds in sight, but Miranda had been in the west long enough to know that a blizzard could come up within a matter of hours, especially in Montana Territory.

Soon, they reached the cabin, and Landry lifted Miranda and the baby down from the wagon and watched them go inside before taking up the reins again and driving the team on toward the barn.

The inside of the house seemed unusually cold, and Miranda made haste to lay Isaiah in his basket, still wrapped in the blanket, so she could build up the fires, first in the stove, then on the hearth. When the place was reasonably warm, she unswaddled the baby and set about the wifely pursuits of lighting lamps and then peeling potatoes and onions to fry for an early supper. Landry meant to go out and search for his boys, but she intended to see that he ate first.

She brewed coffee — an extravagance, since the stuff was usually reserved for breakfast or for entertaining guests — and was adding fresh eggs to the sizzling skillet when Landry finally came in. He looked strained, and his ears and hands were red from the cold.

"I might be away overnight," he warned, taking off his coat and setting the rifle he'd carried to town earlier, beneath the seat of the buckboard, in its rack near the door. He accepted the mug of coffee she'd poured for him with a grateful nod and took a sip right away. His hazel eyes searched her face. "You'll be all right here by yourself?"

She had been alone for much of her life, even when she was in a room full of people, but the idea of Landry being away for a whole night seemed like an almost unbearable ordeal. She couldn't and wouldn't let that response show, of course; he had enough on his mind, with three young boys missing. "I'll be fine. Wash up and stand by the fire for a while, Landry. I'll have your supper ready in just a few minutes."

He nodded again and did as she asked, and when the mixture of potatoes, onions, and eggs was cooked, she served him a plate at the table and sat down to join him. Although it was only midafternoon by then, the days were getting shorter as October progressed toward November, and the first purple-gray shadows of nightfall were already darkening the windows. Now and then, he glanced uneasily toward the now nearly opaque squares of thick glass, no doubt growing more worried with every passing moment.

Miranda figured he was thinking what it would mean to lose Jamie and Marcus, the way he had lost their mother, and just then she could have shaken those boys for frightening him that way. On the other hand, though, she understood why they had done what they had.

"Don't be hard on them," she said quietly. "They're doing the only thing they know to do to help their friend."

Landry's jaw hardened. "Running away from trouble never solved anything. No, ma'am. When I catch up to those little outlaws, they'll be lucky if I don't tan all three of them on the spot."

She felt her eyes widen. "You wouldn't really lay a hand on them — ?"

He huffed out a breath, smiled a sad and rueful smile, and shook his head. "No, but it comforts me some to think of it."

She laughed, though she was as frightened for those three rascally boys as he was. The wind was rising, beginning to howl around the corners of the house, and the fire danced and flickered in the hearth.

Landry finished his food and went to pull on his heavy coat, take down the rifle again, and gather spare ammunition. He went into his room and came out with a bedroll. She stood near the door when he was ready to leave, not quite daring to embrace him as she wanted to do, and whispered, "You'll be careful?"

He took part of a step toward her, or perhaps she just imagined that part. He was looking at her, though, as he raised the wooden latch. "I will. You look out for little Isaiah there, and see you that you don't open that door to anybody you don't know. You'll find a forty-four caliber pistol in the strongbox on the high shelf in that wardrobe in my room. Use it if you see the need."

She swallowed. So far, she'd contrived to avoid laying hand to a firearm, and she did not want to start then. "Do you think — ?"

She couldn't quite bring herself to finish, to ask if Landry expected Mike Houghton to turn up there, looking for Toby.

"There's no telling," Landry answered, when the silence lengthened. "I'll be home as soon as I can. You'll see to the animals if I'm not back by morning?"

She didn't even want to think of Landry not returning before the sun rose, though she knew he probably wouldn't. She simply nodded.

He hesitated — for a moment she thought he would kiss her good-bye, as any husband might do — but in the end he merely told her to fasten the latch behind him and went out, closing the door smartly behind him. Miranda stood there for several long moments, eyes closed, both palms pressed to the rough wooden panel.

Keep him safe, she prayed.

The wind rose still further, as if in answer, and nearly blew out the fire. Miranda bolted the door and turned away.

It made sense to look in at Springwater, to make sure the boys hadn't found their way back there, once the wind came up and the temperature began to drop. Landry rode past the lively Brimstone Saloon, his collar drawn up around his ears and his hat drawn low over his face, making for the station.

Jacob greeted him at the door, and the expression on his weathered face made it clear that he'd been cherishing the same vain hope Landry had — that the boys had given up on their flight and come home. Both men were disappointed.

"No word of them, then?" Jacob asked, stepping back and nodding Landry into the warmth of the Springwater station.

"I was hoping to find them here," Landry admitted. He wouldn't stay long, but neither could he stand on the threshold on a cold night, forcing a friend to hold the door open to an autumn wind. "What about Houghton?"

"He seems content to drink up Trey's liquor over at the Brimstone," Jacob said grimly. "I guess Trey's trying to keep him in sight as long as he can."

Landry nodded. At least he didn't have to worry that Houghton would head out to the ranch and give Miranda any trouble — not yet. He was surprised to realize how much that calmed him, given the fact that his sons were almost certainly in danger, along with young Toby. "I mean to go out looking for them," he told Jacob. "They know this country almost as well as any Blackfoot or Sioux would, though. It won't be easy finding them if they want to stay hidden."

Jacob was reaching for his round black hat and heavy dark coat, both of which hung on sturdy pegs next to the door. "I'll ride along, if you don't mind." He broke loose with something that might have been either a smile or a grimace. "Fact is, I intend to ride along whether you object or not."

Landry knew better than to argue. Jacob was in no condition to go tearing off into the night looking for a trio of wily boys, but he probably knew that without being told. Not that telling him would have done any good.

June-bug appeared from the rear corridor, hands bunched into fists in her apron pockets. "You have a care, Jacob Mc-Caffrey," she said. "I can't spare you, and that's a fact."

The big man crossed the room, kissed his wife's upturned face. "I'll be fine," he assured her. "And if I have my way, so will those boys." He stroked her cheek with a gentle pass of knuckles as gnarled as the roots of an old tree. "You tend to the prayin'. Don't you give the Lord a moment's peace until we've got young Toby and the Kildare boys back home safe, you hear?"

She smiled, her eyes overly bright. "Yes, Jacob," she said. "I hear."

The night outside was bitter cold, and the wind was sharp as the prongs of a new pitchfork, but Jacob had his big mule saddled in the time it took to whistle twice and spit, and Landry welcomed his presence, even if he wasn't one to say much of anything. Thus the two men rode in easy silence, each one keeping his own counsel.

Miranda stayed busy for a while, feeding and bathing the baby, rocking him to sleep, clearing up the dishes, and banking the fire. After she'd bedded Isaiah down in his basket, she tried to settle at the table, with the reading primer Rachel had given her to study on, but she couldn't concentrate and that made it hard to pin the words down to where they made sense.

She rose and went to the window, once, twice, a third time. She hoped to see her stepsons, and poor Toby, and of course Landry. Without Jamie and Marcus, without her husband, that modest house seemed huge and very empty.

Eventually, she gave up and went to bed, but she heard every coyote, every change in the wind, every creak of the house's heavy wooden walls and tightly laid floors. After several hours of tossing and turning, Miranda got up and, carrying Isaiah and his basket, took herself off to Landry's room. She had no right to be there, wife or none, but her longing for him was an ache, soul-deep, and she could no longer ignore it. Boldly, she set Isaiah down close at hand, then threw back the covers and climbed right into Landry's bed.

The sheets smelled deliciously of him, a unique combination of fresh grass and sun-dried linens and hard-working man, and it was a comfort to lie where he had lain, to rest her head on his pillow. She would make the bed up in the morning, she promised herself, as she finally began the long, slow tumble toward the solace of sleep, and he would never know she'd been there.

"Pa! Over here, Pa — come quick!"

The voice was Jamie's, and the panicked sound of it wrenched Landry's breathing to a painful stop in his throat. Still, he spurred his horse forward, knew the direction to take. Jacob kept pace, and it was he who called out, "We're comin', boy!"

Jamie stumbled out of the brush, teeth chattering, face bloodied and scratched. "Pa, Mr. McCaffrey — it's Toby. He's bad hurt. We figured to hide in our cave — that one you showed us when we was huntin' bear last year — and Toby fell a long way —"

When Landry leaned down to offer his younger son a hand, Jamie took it and sprang onto the horse behind him, agile as a monkey. "It's up ahead there, through that little draw. Marcus is with him. We covered him up with a blanket, but we was — were — scairt to move him."

"You did right," Landry said. They'd discuss the drawbacks of running off some other time, when all three boys were safe.

Jacob was the first to reach the place where the boy lay, and he was off the mule and crouched on the ground next to him before Landry had even dismounted. A kerosene lantern, no doubt purloined from the barn at home, glowed next to the prone figure of Toby and the kneeling one of Landry's elder son.

"Tell me where it hurts, boy," Jacob said, and Landry felt a sweep of relief. Until then, he hadn't known whether or not the lad was conscious. "We're here now, Landry and me, and we're going to take you back home. Doc Parrish will fix you up neat and tidy."

Drawing near, Landry saw that Toby had a broken leg. Marcus, white with fear for his friend, looked up at his father with a plea in his eyes.

Landry simply held out his arm, and as quick as that, he had a son on either side, clinging to him as if to keep from toppling over the edge of a cliff.

"We didn't figure on Toby getting hurt, Pa," Marcus said.

Landry squeezed his son's thin but widening shoulders. They'd be men all too soon, his boys. They were growing up fast. "I know you didn't," he said. He addressed his next words to Jacob, who was running practiced hands over Toby's ribs, checking for more injuries. Until Pres Parrish came to Springwater, Jacob had been the closest thing to a doctor they had. "Is it all right to move him?"

Jacob didn't look up. He was gazing down into Toby's dirt-smudged, bruised face. "I reckon so," he answered, "but it's going to hurt some. You understand that, don't you, boy?"

Toby nodded. Then Jacob lifted him off the ground in both arms, blanket and all, and his face reflected the child's agony when Toby cried out from the pain. "Hand him up to me," Jacob said, offering the boy to Landry, who held him while his friend mounted and then bent to recover his burden.

"Fetch that lantern," Landry said to Marcus, when his sons' spotted pony ambled out of the bushes, dragging its reins, "and we'll follow Jacob into Springwater."

Marcus nodded, picked up the light, and scrambled onto the pony's back.

"You gonna whip us when we get home, Pa?" Jamie asked. For once, he seemed younger than Marcus, which he was.

"I ought to," Landry replied. He was worried about Toby still, and about Jacob as well, but at the same time he was as thankful for finding his boys safe as he had ever been for anything.

"Will you?" Marcus wanted to know. He'd brought the pony alongside Landry's gelding.

"I've never done it before," he said, after keeping a judicious silence for a while. "I don't reckon I'll start now. But don't go thinking you won't be punished for this, because you will. That was a damn fool thing you did."

Jacob and Toby and the mule were ahead, riding through the thin moonlight toward the warmth and safety of Springwater, and Landry saw no reason to keep pace. He reckoned, though, that he'd never forget the look of Jacob McCaffrey when he'd lifted that boy up into his arms and gathered him close against his broad chest.

He was worth ten of Mike Houghton, if you asked Landry Kildare.

Chapter

6

It took Miranda a long, sleep-fuddled moment to realize that the man looming at the foot of the bed wasn't Landry, and when she did, the awareness brought her breathing to a hard stop and nearly did the same to her heart. She suppressed an urge to raise herself onto her elbows and peer through the thick darkness; better to pretend she was still asleep. Recalling the .44 Landry had told her about before he left the house, she wished she'd taken the time to get the pistol down and set it within reach on the bedside table.

"Where's your man?" Mike Houghton demanded. He knew, then, that she was awake; she'd most likely gasped aloud when she saw him.

"How did you get in here?" Miranda countered. She'd latched the door and checked all the windows before retiring, and she would have heard any attempt at breaking in.

Houghton chuckled. He was a huge, featureless shadow in the gloom, but Miranda could see his bulky outline clearly enough, and catch the brew of sour smells coming off his skin and clothes. "Came up through the root cellar," he said, with a degree of pride. "Now, like I asked you before, where's that man of yours?"

Miranda wet her lips with the tip of her tongue, stalling. She was in powerful trouble, she knew that, but it was little Isaiah she was afraid for; all her instincts were geared toward protecting him. "He went out looking for his sons," she said finally, when she was afraid the intruder might finally round the end of the bed and come at her. "I reckon he'll be back any time now."

Houghton heaved a sigh. He'd obviously thought Miranda and Landry were hiding Toby themselves, had him secreted away in the cabin someplace. Probably, he'd already searched every nook and cranny.

Miranda wondered when she'd gotten to be such a heavy sleeper; the slightest peep from Isaiah invariably awakened her instantly. Houghton was a big man, and not particularly graceful, so he'd surely made some noise. She guessed she'd been extra tired from the strain of the past few days.

"I'm getting real weary of dealing with you people," Toby's so-called father said, with another sigh, this one sounding long-suffering and much put-upon. "I reckon I'll just have myself a seat at your table and wait for your husband to get home. You get up and make me something to eat. I'm starving."

Miranda was at once relieved that Houghton didn't mean to force himself on her, at least not right away, and very frightened of the reception Landry would get when he returned, unsuspecting, almost certainly bringing the boys with him. Eager to get the unwanted visitor as far away from her baby as she could, Miranda spoke firmly. "You go on out and sit down at the table. I'll be right out to build up the fire."

Houghton started toward the gaping doorway — thanks to Landry's thoroughness, the hinges hadn't even squeaked when he entered — then paused and turned back to face Miranda. She saw him extend one beefy arm and shake a finger at her, even though she couldn't make out his features in the dark. "Don't you try nothin', either," he warned. "You come through this here door with, say, a gun in your hand, I'm going to be ready for you, and that man of yours will meet with a sorry mess when he comes in."

Miranda felt a chill hand-spring down her spine. She knew he meant what he said; she'd have to find another opportunity to fetch that .44 down from the wardrobe shelf, and she'd have to do it soon, if she wanted to get the better of Mike Houghton. Landry had said it was in a strongbox; did that mean it was locked? Surely, with young boys in the house, and both of them reckless little rascals, it must be. Where, then, was the key? "I just want to wrap up in something warm. There's a bite in the air."

She heard a pistol cock, saw a flash of moonlight on the barrel, icy cold and blue-black. "I don't want no foolishness," Houghton growled.

She nodded, unable, for the moment, to speak. He must have seen, because he grunted and turned to lumber out of the room.

Miranda paused to draw a deep breath in an effort to calm her racing thoughts and figure out what to do. In the end, there was nothing much she *could* do, besides put on a wrapper, fix Houghton a meal, and hope to God that Landry wouldn't stumble in and get himself shot to death, right in front of her and his boys.

Help me, she prayed, and hurried down the way to her own room to fetch a wrapper she'd seen folded in one of the bureau drawers. The garment had been Caroline's, of course, and Landry probably wouldn't appreciate her wearing it, but for now there was no choice. If he didn't understand, well, she reckoned that was his problem.

When she reached the cabin's main room, Houghton had made himself at home, lighting the lamps, settling in Landry's chair at the table, bold as brass. He was smoking Landry's pipe, too.

Miranda calculated her chances of braining him with the fireplace poker before he managed to pick up the big hog-leg of a gun he'd laid beside the kerosene lantern in the center of the table and decided they were unfavorable.

She went to the stove instead, made a lot of clatter opening doors, stirring embers, stuffing in kindling and chunks of wood. Only when she had a good snapping fire going did she turn to look at Mike Houghton. He ran his gaze over her in a way that made her skin shrink back and quaver against her bones.

"You said you were hungry," she reminded him, pretending to a bravery she didn't really feel. Landry was sure to show up soon, and there was the baby to think about, and the boys. What was she going to do? "What do you want?" she demanded.

He ran his eyes over her once more, eyes that put her in mind of that old boar hog Landry had shot just the day before yesterday. They had the same black-hearted glint in them, the same evil intentions. "Now that, little lady, just depends on how long that man of yours stays gone. I've got business with him, right enough, but I think maybe I might have some with you, too." He paused, chewing on the stem of Landry's pipe, filling the air with tobacco smoke and the general stench of his own person. "For now, some hotcakes would do. Bacon, too, if you can scrounge some up, and five or six eggs."

Miranda nodded, hands on her hips. "You'll have your bacon and hotcakes and all. Then you better just ride out, because if my husband finds you here, he's likely to kill you deader than the Confederacy. You may not have noticed, Mr. Houghton," she put just the slightest emphasis on the *Mr.*, "but you aren't welcome at Springwater. Toby is one of us now, and you ought to leave him right where he's been since you left him."

"I listened to the preacher's sermon this morning," Houghton said. "I don't need one from you, too. Just make me them eggs and a stack of hotcakes about that high." He indicated a sizable height between his two hands. "A pound or two of pork, too. And some coffee. I've had me a mite too much whiskey in there at the Brimstone Saloon. Hell of a thing if I was to pass out."

That, Miranda thought, was too much to hope for. She went to the pantry, returned with the flour and other ingredients she needed. While in the pantry, she nearly tripped over the rag rug on the floor, and hastily smoothed it with one foot. Then she eyed the butcher knives, aligned in a neat row in a handmade rack, as was typical of Landry, but she ruled out the idea of using one against Houghton almost as soon as it came to her mind. He'd shoot her dead before she took the first swipe at that filthy hide of his.

She stirred the hotcake batter with unusual vigor, her mind going as fast as the spoon in her hand, but achieving a whole lot less.

"What I don't see," Houghton confided to her stiff back, sounding genuinely puzzled, "is why you folks around here think so highly of that boy of mine. He's just like his mother — and she was no better than she should be. A whore, down New Orleans way. He ever tell you that? He's got her looks and her crafty mind. Can't trust him any further than you can throw a mule."

Miranda straightened her already-straight spine and turned to glare at the man, the bowl of batter clasped in both arms and propped against her middle. "Why do you insist on taking him away, if you feel that way about him? He's been happy here. The McCaffreys love him like their own. He goes to school and to church. What could you possibly want with one skinny little boy, when it's plain you don't give a hoot or a holler what happens to him and probably never have?" She wasn't just talking to Mike Houghton, she realized. She was talking to her own father, who had been equally worthless, and absent even when he was in the same room with her.

"We — I need him to help me with some honest work," Houghton all but whined. "He might be just a boy, but he can earn a man's wages."

Miranda set the big iron skillet on the stove with a bang and lobbed in some lard from the grease jar Landry kept on top of the warming oven on the stove. "You and I both know he can't do any such thing," she snapped. "You want to make him into an outlaw and a saddle-tramp, that's all."

For a moment, she thought she might have gone a step too far. Houghton's whiskey-reddened face grew even more flushed, and his boarlike eyes narrowed until they were almost gone. "It ain't none of your concern *what* I make out of that boy, now is it? He's mine, and I can do with him what I want."

"For God's sake," Miranda spat, furious beyond all good sense, "he's not a mule or a half-starved dog, he's a boy, a human being with a heart and a soul and a mind, same as everybody else. He belongs to himself and the good Lord, and besides that, you gave up any claim a long time ago when you left him alone in the woods to fend for himself!"

Somewhat to Miranda's surprise, Houghton didn't pick up the pistol and shoot her. He seemed taken aback by her accusation, if only briefly, even anxious to prove himself without guilt. "I meant to get back afore I did," he said. "I ran into some trouble, that's all."

The sun was beginning to lighten the gloom at the windows. Landry would be home soon. *Come quickly,* she pleaded silently. *Stay away.* "What sort of trouble?" she asked, without sympathy. "Jail, maybe?"

Houghton looked pained and not a little insulted. "You ain't very respectful, you know that? I've got half a mind to backhand you, teach you a lesson."

"You lay a hand on me, and I'll kill you," Miranda said. She didn't know where the words had come from, they just tumbled out of her mouth all on their own, but they were gospel-true, each one.

Houghton laughed. "You? You ain't hardly bigger than that boy of mine." His expression turned to a speculative leer. "But you are a pretty thing, I vow. Right sweet-smellin'. Warm, too, I reckon, and soft in all the right places."

Just the thought of Houghton laying hands on her made bile rush into the back of Miranda's throat, but she wasn't going to let him know she was scared if she could keep from it. "Here," she said, and served him a plate of food with a slam of the plate against the tabletop. "Eat and get out."

She watched his face while he weighed the urgings of a naturally mean spirit against what was probably an insatiable appetite for food. In the end, to Miranda's well-hidden relief, he chose the victuals. While Houghton ate, Miranda listened for Landry's horse and hoped to high heaven she wouldn't wind up a widow before she ever got a chance to be a real wife.

Upon reaching Springwater, Landry hurried to fetch Doc Parrish while Jacob took

Toby into the station, with some help from Jamie and Marcus. When Landry returned with Pres, they found the boy lying on one of the tables in the main room. June-bug was doing her best to comfort Toby, but it was plain that he was suffering. Little wonder; part of the big bone in the youngster's thigh was protruding right through the torn fabric of his pants.

Landry looked away, and swallowed hard once before looking back.

"Everybody out of the way," Doc Parrish said, practically as soon as he'd cleared the threshold. Most likely, Landry reflected, nobody had ever accused the man of mincing words.

Jamie and Marcus were already huddled in a corner, the freckles standing out on their pasty white faces. Landry reckoned he ought to haul them both to the nearest woodshed and raise a few blisters on their backsides — that was what his own pa would have done — but he couldn't bring himself to do it. It just didn't seem right to him, beating on another human being, especially ones you loved.

Jacob and June-bug weren't about to leave the boy, no matter what the Doc said, and the expressions on their faces made it plain. However, they did make way for him.

Pres's voice was remarkably calm as he bent over Toby to examine what had to be the worst break Landry had ever seen. No doubt the Doc had seen worse, though, given that he'd served as a field surgeon in the war. "Looks like you fell off a mountain," he said cheerfully.

The boy's face was pale as death and popping sweat, but he worked up a crooked grin all the same. "Yes, sir," he said. "I reckon I dropped twenty or thirty feet afore I hit the ground."

Pres put the ends of his stethoscope into his ears and listened thoughtfully to Toby's heart. "Well, that was a damn fool thing to do," said the Doc. "Now you and I and especially the McCaffreys here are in for a long night." He let the stethoscope dangle from his neck and popped open his beat-up doctor bag. "You're in shock," he continued, still speaking to Toby, although he raised his eyes and met first Jacob's gaze and then June-bug's, over the boy's head. He looked down at Toby again. "That's why I can't use ether or chloroform to put you to sleep. I'm going to give you a dose of laudanum, though, and that'll take the edge off. Once I've wrestled that leg bone of yours back where it belongs — and that's going to hurt like hell, Toby, and there's no

139

point in telling you otherwise — I'll sew you up and put on a splint. Long about that time, you ought to be able to swallow some more medicine and have a good, long rest. Fair enough?"

Young Toby clenched his jaw against pain that was already pretty fierce — had to be right up against the edge of unbearable, in fact — and nodded his head. "Fair enough," he agreed staunchly. It made Landry's heart ache, seeing such a little kid suffer like that, no matter that he'd brought the whole thing on himself, with some help from Jamie and Marcus.

"We're thankful to you," Jacob said to Landry. He was still standing at the end of the table where Toby lay, one of the child's hands pressed between his own. "You'd best be getting those boys of yours home now. Your bride will be watching the road."

His bride.

Miranda hadn't been far from the forefront of Landry's mind the whole of the night, for all that had happened. He longed to see with his own eyes that she was all right, to simply be under the same roof with her again. He wondered if the strange mingling of tenderness and almost ferocious desire she stirred in him — he was ready to admit to such feelings, at least in the privacy of his own mind — was the beginning of love. He just didn't know, since he'd never felt exactly this way before, even with Caroline. By comparison, though, his feelings for Miranda were richer, deeper, and more powerful, the emotions a man held for a woman. Knowing Caroline from his boyhood, he'd loved her as a youth loves his sweetheart, with a certain shallow innocence.

"You're sure we won't be needed," Landry said. The question came out sounding like a statement instead. He was too worn-out to go putting a lot of inflection in his words.

A corner of Jacob's mouth lifted slightly in what might have been an inclination toward a smile. "You came in mighty handy tonight, my friend, but I believe it's Doc here we need now. You go on home. We know where to send if there's call to do it."

Landry nodded a farewell at Jacob, then at June-bug. The Doc was occupied, as he should have been, with Toby's leg, having already dragged off his coat and pushed up his sleeves. Savannah joined them, began heating water on the stove without even being asked. When Landry turned to summon his sons, they were already on their feet and wearing their jackets.

"You want us to stay, Toby?" Jamie asked, peering at his friend but carefully avoiding looking at his injured leg. Landry couldn't really blame his son; it was a nasty sight, all that torn flesh and splintered bone. It was sure to take the Doc a long while to put it all back together the way the Lord had it in the first place.

"You go on," Toby answered. "I'll look for you tomorrow, though."

"We'll be here," Marcus assured him, from Jamie's side. Then he glanced up at Landry. "If our pa will let us leave the ranch, anyhow."

Landry didn't make it easy on them. "Fetch the horses," he said.

Three-quarters of an hour later, the ranch house was in sight, and Landry felt some surprise to see that the windows were alight. Granted, it was nearly sunup, but in his brief experience, Miranda wasn't an early riser. He was usually up, with the coffee brewing, before she stirred from the spare room.

"Pa," Jamie hissed. He was riding behind Marcus now, on the pony. "Look there, behind Ma's oak trees."

Landry felt his heart flatten out and roll right up into the back of his throat. Sure enough, there in the midst of the trees Caroline had raised from acorns gathered back home in Missouri before they headed west, was an unfamiliar horse, still saddled and grazing. Mike Houghton's horse, he'd be willing to bet; he didn't recognize it as belonging to any of the men around Springwater.

"You suppose he done hurt her, Pa?" Jamie asked. He sounded plaintive.

"Stay here," Landry said, drawing his rifle from the scabbard affixed to his saddle and swinging down off the gelding's back. How the hell had Houghton gotten in, he wondered, as he ran over the situation mentally. He'd bolted the windows himself, and he'd heard the bolt fall into place behind him a few seconds after he'd closed the door to go looking for the boys.

"Pa," Marcus insisted. "He's mean. Toby swears he killed his ma, made her drink poison. He might shoot you."

"Do as I told you," Landry whispered. "Stay put and don't make any noise." Just then, one of the horses neighed, and he could only hope Houghton would think it was his own.

"But, Pa — how you gonna get in there?" Jamie asked. He was beside Landry, that fast, and had caught hold of his sleeve. "He might hurt Miranda — or you — or the baby. You've got to sneak up on him."

"How the devil am I going to do that?" Landry snapped. He was asking himself and God that question, more than the boy.

"Through the root cellar," Jamie said. He gulped and glanced at Marcus once; obviously, he'd just betrayed a closely guarded secret.

"I sealed the doors to that root cellar a long time ago," he said, growing impatient now, anxious to see that Miranda and little Isaiah were safe. He wouldn't be able to breathe right until he knew they hadn't been harmed.

Jamie swallowed again. "Me and Marcus fixed them so we could go in and out that way, without you knowing. I reckon that's how Houghton got into the house, too."

Landry swore under his breath and started to the other side of the cabin in a half crouch. Entering through the old cellar, he could come up into the pantry through a trap door. Soon as he got under the house, he could hear Houghton's voice overhead.

"That was a mighty fine breakfast, missus," he was saying. "Now you come on over here and sit down on my lap."

Landry set his jaw and concentrated on lifting the trap door quietly enough to keep from attracting Houghton's attention and thus getting his head blown off. This was no time to make a mistake.

"No," he heard Miranda say firmly. "I made you the food you wanted. Now you just get out of here before my husband comes home and shoots you for a scoundrel."

Landry eased the door up, reached through and laid his rifle soundlessly on the pantry floor, then climbed up after it.

"You ain't gonna make me turn mean, are you, little lady?" Houghton drawled. "I'd hate to make my point by going in that bedroom, fetching that baby of yours, and —"

"You touch my child," Miranda broke in, "you just lay one of your filthy paws on him, and I'll see you spend a good long time dyin'."

Houghton laughed, and his voice took on an oily, cajoling note. Landry's hands flexed spasmodically around the rifle; he'd never wanted to shoot anybody down in cold blood before that moment, but he was ready to kill this sorry excuse for a man without waiting for another heartbeat to pass. For Miranda's sake, and the baby's, he made himself wait, slipped to the doorway of the pantry.

There was a lantern burning on the worktable beside the stove, and Landry cast a glance over the floor to make sure he wasn't throwing a shadow. He saw Miranda's reflection in the glass of the window across the room, and Houghton's, along with the faintest suggestion of his own, and held his breath.

Miranda was standing only a few feet from Houghton's chair, and she was directly in the line of fire between the center of that bastard's heart and Landry's rifle. He willed his wife to step aside, willed it so hard that for a moment he was afraid he'd actually spoken aloud.

A horse nickered outside.

"What's that?" Houghton asked. He was quick, that one.

Miranda's arms were folded. "I reckon it was a horse," she said, and if she was afraid, there was nothing in her voice to indicate as much. "My husband's back, I guess. You'd better start saying your prayers."

Under any other circumstances, her audacity would have made Landry smile. As it was, he was too worried about keeping her alive to be amused. He knew he cared for her, that was plain by the way his gut was wound up around itself, but they'd sort that out later, when he'd dealt with Houghton.

Houghton went toward the window, taking the pistol with him. That must have been when he saw Landry's almost transparent image in the glass.

He whirled and in an instant the air was singing with bullets, Landry's, and Houghton's as well. Landry heard Miranda scream, heard the baby wailing in fright somewhere nearby, watched as the other man dropped to the floor, bleeding from the shoulder.

Landry was wounded himself; he wasn't sure where, though he'd bet on his ribs being cracked, and didn't give a damn. He crossed to Houghton and kicked the handgun out of his reach.

Miranda stood staring at him, both hands pressed to her mouth, her eyes big as pie tins. "You're shot," she sobbed. "Oh, Landry, you've been shot —"

"Hush," he said, as Jamie and Marcus poured into the room from the pantry, having entered, as Landry had, through the root cellar. Marcus picked up Houghton's gun and held it on him. He was face-down on the floor, bleeding copiously, moaning and just beginning to pull himself up toward consciousness.

Miranda flung herself at Landry then, hurtled right into his arms, like a little cannonball, and he held her, even though it hurt. Held her tight. *Thank you,* he said to God, in the silence of his heart.

"Did he hurt you?" Landry asked, with

the next breath. "Or the baby?"

She shook her head, her beautiful violet eyes brimming with tears. Landry would never forget the way she'd held up tonight; she had more courage than a lot of the men he'd known in his life. "But you're *shot*," she sniffled insistently. Poor little Isaiah was still howling.

"What should we do, Pa?" Marcus asked.

He didn't so much as glance in the boy's direction. "One of you tie up that polecat, hand and foot. Make sure he can't get loose. The other, head for Springwater and bring back Trey Hargreaves."

Just that morning, before church — Lord, it seemed like a lifetime ago — Landry and the other men had made an agreement that Trey would serve as a sort of unofficial lawman, just until they managed to rope in a real one. He'd been chosen because he had steady hands and a mean streak, as well as a storeroom with no windows and a door three inches thick.

"Let me look at you," Miranda said, stepping back at last, pulling Landry's shirt out of his trousers, clawing at the buttons. "Look at all this blood —"

The room swam around him, seemed to undulate, like a heat mirage in the field. He caught both his wife's frantic hands in his, stayed her from undressing him right there. "Miranda," he said.

She swallowed convulsively and stared up at him, speechless. He felt her shivering. "Wh-what?" she asked, after a long time.

"Go get that baby before he brings the roof down with his hollering," Landry said. Then he let go of her, sat down in his chair at the table, and did his level best not to pass out from the pain.

7

By the time Trey came to fetch Mike Houghton, bringing an exhausted Doc Parrish with him, the sun was high and Miranda had already cleaned Landry's side wound and bound his ribs up good and tight with an old sheet torn into strips. He was asleep in his own bed.

The Doc came in and examined him, first thing, while Miranda hovered nearby, twisting her hands. Landry awakened and grinned wanly.

"Hello, Pres. How's Toby?"

Doc smiled. "He'll be fine in six weeks or so. Young bones heal quickly." He cast a re-assuring, sidelong glance at Miranda, and that eased her mind. "Near as I can tell, this bride of yours did a good job fixing you up. That's a flesh wound you've got there. Your ribs are a little the worse for wear, though. You'll have to take it easy for a while. No heavy work."

Landry tried to sit up in protest. "I've got a field to plow under —"

"I guess it'll just have to wait," the Doc said, in dismissive tones. "Now I'd better go out there and have a look at that fellow your boys have got hog-tied on the floor." With that, he went out.

Landry looked pale, lying there against his pillows, but handsome, with his rumpled brown hair, new beard, and soft, expressive eyes. While she was undressing him, her thoughts had been anything but romantic, but now that the danger was past, well, it made her warm inside to remember. He extended one hand to her.

"Come here," he said.

She went to him, sat down carefully on the side of the bed. All of the sudden, her throat was so tight and dry that she couldn't speak, didn't even dare to try.

"Looks like we might have to put off that honeymoon in Choteau for a while," he said gently, "but we'll go, Miranda. I promise you that. Before winter sets in."

She had to blink back tears; she loved him so much, and she'd come so close to losing him. The slightest turn of Houghton's wrist, just a hair's breadth to the left, and that bullet would have gone straight into Landry's heart instead of creasing his ribs. She and all three of her boys would have been alone.

"I love you," she blurted out. She shouldn't have said it aloud, she supposed, but she hadn't been able to help it any more than she could help drawing her next breath.

He was still holding her hand, and he raised it to his mouth, ran her knuckles lightly across his lips. His eyes were warm, with a tender look in them that affected her just the way a summer sky did, when it was a mite too blue to be borne. "I love you, too," he said quietly. "I knew that when I saw Houghton's horse tied up out there last night and realized that I might lose you. We can build on what we feel, Miranda, if you're willing to give me, oh, say, fifty years of your life." He grinned impishly. "Starting right now."

Having said that, he drew her down and kissed her soundly, for the first time, right on the mouth. It made Miranda feel as though she'd just sat herself down on a shaft of lightning, spearing upwards through her vitals and exploding in the center of her soul like fireworks.

She was gasping when he released her, and surely flushed, too, since her blood felt hot. "My goodness," she said. Tom had never kissed her like that; she'd remember if he had. Not that she could rightly recall what he'd looked like, let alone how it was when he touched her. He might have been somebody she'd heard about in a story, for all the substance of his memory.

Landry laughed, but his expression was ever-so-tender. He traced the outline of Miranda's jaw with the tip of one index finger. "You move your things in here when you get a chance, Mrs. Kildare. You'll be sleeping with me tonight, and every night after this."

Miranda felt a swell of joy and anticipation. She didn't figure Landry could manage much in the way of lovemaking, laid up like that, but just lying beside him, like a real wife, would be pure bliss to her. She nodded shyly.

Landry reached past her, to the bedside table, and when he drew back his hand, she saw that he was holding the wedding picture he'd taken with Caroline, so long before. He seemed to be bidding the image a silent farewell, then he held it out to Miranda. "The boys will want this one day. Will you put it aside for them?"

Again, Miranda couldn't speak. She nodded, trying not to cry.

Landry cupped her chin in one hand and

ran the callused pad of his thumb across her mouth, setting her insides on fire all over again. His grin was both rascally and gentle. "Don't," he chided softly. "I'll never give you reason to weep. You have my word on that."

She leaned forward, let her forehead rest against his chest. It was a while before she could bring herself under control. "I'll do you proud, Landry. I promise I will."

He touched her lips again, made her want him, and desperately, as easily as that. "You already have," he said.

"I can't read too well," she confessed. She didn't want to mislead him, make him think she was smarter than she was.

"I'll help you," he said.

That was when Miranda knew for sure that everything was going to be all right, that, together, she and Landry would build a love with walls as thick and sturdy as any castle in faraway England. It might take time, it might take effort, but it would rise against the sky to stand forever, providing shelter and solace to them and to all their children, born and unborn.

When Mike Houghton had been locked up in Trey's storeroom for a solid ten days, the U.S. Marshal came out from Choteau to collect him. He'd been implicated in half a dozen holdups, Houghton had, and the lawman said it was likely he'd be in jail for a long stretch. Long enough, it was safe to assume, for Toby to grow up and become his own man.

In the meantime, of course, he would remain with the McCaffreys. Somewhere along the line, he'd taken to calling Jacob "Pa," and June-bug "Mama." Nobody corrected him, and Jacob was like a new man, gaining weight, preaching a rousing sermon that first Sunday after the marshal took Mike Houghton away.

Winter was coming, and the snows would be upon them soon, but the people of Springwater were in high spirits, almost giddy with relief. Whatever affected one of their number, for good or for ill, affected all of them, in one way or another. They were a unit, a family, and growing fast.

Miranda stood with her husband that blustery day, Landry using a cane but already much recovered. The preaching was over, and they were waiting for the stagecoach. Its approach was clearly audible in the near distance, even over the excited talk of the folks gathered to bid Mr. and Mrs. Kildare Godspeed on their honeymoon trip to Choteau. Miranda, clad almost entirely in borrowed clothes, was so excited she could barely keep from dancing for joy. She had never in her life made any kind of journey just for the sake of pleasure.

Savannah, eyes bright with happiness at the prospect, was to keep Isaiah, who had taken well to the bottle, and Marcus and Jamie, somewhat subdued — Miranda was sure it was only temporary — since their latest brush with disaster, would stay right there at Springwater station, with Jacob and June-bug. Landry had promised them a memorable hiding if they got into any kind of trouble while he and Miranda were away, and since he'd laid one hand on a Bible when he said it, everybody knew he'd keep his word, even though he was not a man to administer harsh punishment.

Finally, the stage came, and it was empty, except for Guffy O'Hagan, the driver. He was a big man, with hair the color of ground ginger and eyes as brown and gentle as a deer's. Even though he actually lived in Choteau, everybody at Springwater considered him one of them.

"Well, then," Guffy boomed, remaining high up in the box, reins in hand, as Landry helped Miranda into the coach, as fancily as if they were two storybook people about to take an airing in a golden carriage. "So I've got me a pair of passengers after all. Thought I'd be making this run alone for sure."

Landry paused to grin up at him, then hoisted himself into the coach and sat beside Miranda, laying his cane on the opposite seat. Ever since they'd declared themselves, one to the other, Miranda had shared Landry's bed, but they hadn't done much besides some kissing and the kind of touching that made the blood sing but never quite satisfied. Now, Landry was almost well, he'd made that plain in a hundred ways, and when they'd gotten to the hotel in Choteau and locked the door of their room behind them, he meant to make love to her. For real.

The trip did not pass quickly; it was a long, rough road from Springwater to Choteau, but Landry and Miranda had a great deal to talk about. They worked out how many children they'd like to have — three more, all girls — and what they ought to plant in the field Tom Bellweather and Scully Wainwright had plowed under for him while he was laid up. There were long silences, too, times when they just looked out the windows and watched the countryside jostle by, thinking their own thoughts, and that was as comfortable as the talking.

Some men, Miranda knew, might have taken advantage of being alone with their wives in a moving stagecoach, but Landry was a gentleman. It wasn't, he told her, eyes twinkling with affection and mischief, that he didn't want to strip her to the skin and learn every part of her. He'd do that on the way back, if they had the coach to themselves again, he warned, but he wanted their first time to be a little more leisurely and a lot more comfortable. He wanted to have her on a bed, he said, and he told her in great detail what he meant to do, and even outlined how she would respond.

By the time they finally pulled into town, when it was nearly nightfall, Miranda could barely keep from squirming, she was so aroused.

The stagecoach stopped in front of the National Hotel, where a man with a young and very nervous wife was waiting to board. Miranda overheard the man telling Guffy that their name was Barnes, and they were on their way to Springwater to start up a newspaper. They had equipment and a stake to put up a building, though they meant to winter over at the coach station run by some people name of McCaffrey.

Miranda smiled to herself as her husband squired her toward the open doors of the hotel. Jacob was right; Springwater *was* growing, and a newspaper would probably draw a lot of new settlers. They would make a point when they got back home, she knew, of paying a call at the station to welcome the Barneses.

The lobby of the hotel would have been rugged by Savannah's standards, Miranda thought, and especially by Rachel's, but to her it looked like a grand palace, with its horsehair settees, potted plants, and long wooden registration desk. Blushing a little, eyes downcast — surely everyone must know that she and Landry were on their honeymoon, about to go upstairs and, well, be there. Upstairs. Alone together.

She swallowed hard. *Don't let me faint,* she prayed.

In good time, Landry had the key to their room, number forty-four, at the back, as requested in Mr. Kildare's letter, the clerk said, and Landry took Miranda by the arm and squired her toward the stairway. He must have felt just fine, because he didn't even seem to realize that he'd left his cane behind, propped against the desk where he'd signed the guest book with a flourish. *Mr. and Mrs. Landry T. Kildare, Springwater.*

The room itself was small, dominated by a large brass bed, but the spread looked clean and the sheets, white and clean, had hardly been mended. Miranda took notice of that when, as soon as a boy had brought their satchel up from downstairs and left with a nickel for his trouble, Landry immediately drew back the covers. He hadn't even taken off his hat yet.

Miranda stood stiffly in the center of the room, which still put her within her husband's easy reach, since she could almost have touched any one of the four walls from right there. Landry's eyes, usually full of lively humor, smouldered now, they seared Miranda's flesh wherever his gaze lit — at the hollow of her throat, on her mouth, on her full breasts, which were practically back to normal, since she'd stopped nursing Isaiah. Practically. They were still unusually sensitive.

Landry tossed aside his good, go-to-preaching hat, then his one and only suit coat. He was unfastening his celluloid collar, which he hated with a passion usually reserved for the territorial governor, when he finally spoke.

"Get out of those clothes, Mrs. Kildare, and let me look at you."

Miranda wanted him to look, wanted him to touch — with all her heart, she *did* — but she was nervous. What if he found her lacking in some way — in a thousand ways? She didn't know much about lovemaking, or about pleasing a man, for all her supposed experience. Tom hadn't expected her to do anything but lie there while he strained over her.

Trembling a little, she untied the ribbons that held her bonnet in place, and set it aside. Took off her cloak.

"Let down your hair first," Landry said hoarsely, when she moved to undo the buttons at the front of her bodice. He'd stopped undressing after removing his shirt, to reveal the bindings still tightly wrapped around his middle, and his suspenders were hanging in loops at his sides.

Miranda raised her arms, pulled the pins out of her hair, so that it tumbled, heavy and rich, around her shoulders.

Landry made a growling sound and took a step toward her, and that was far enough, because there hadn't been much space between them in the first place. He pulled her close, held her against his hard chest, and bent his head to take her mouth with his own.

Knowing there would be no stopping, that this time they would truly become one flesh, set Miranda's blood afire. She moaned as Landry deepened the kiss, at the same time finding her breasts, weighing them in his strong, working man's hands. He smelled deliciously of laundry starch, sunshine, and — even though it was early November — summer grass.

Nimbly, as though he'd practiced the motions in his mind a thousand times beforehand, he opened the front of her dress without breaking the breathless kiss, and Miranda felt a sweet, fierce catch, somewhere down deep, when he broke away to look into her eyes.

"You'll have to lie down," he said, with a slanted and roguish grin, "because I can't bend to kiss those breasts of yours, and that's something I've got to do."

She couldn't speak, just stood there while he stripped away her dress, her camisole and petticoats, leaving her in just her drawers, stockings and shoes. She'd intended to wear a corset, to trim her waist to a fashionable size, but Landry had forbidden that. She was never going to own anything with spikes in it, let alone wear it, he'd said, and that was the end of the discussion.

Now, he knelt, like the prince trying the glass slipper on Cinderella's foot, untied Miranda's laces and pulled off her shoes. Rolled her stockings down, slowly, slowly, over her thighs and knees, calves and ankles.

Everywhere he touched her, with just the lightest pass of his fingers, seemed to leap with a pulse all its own.

He coaxed her to stand, in murmured words, when he'd taken away everything but her bloomers, and she felt his breath through the thin fabric and groaned when he kissed her there, in that most private place, then nipped at her lightly with his teeth.

She let her head fall back, surrendered without protest when he removed the drawers, too, and parted the nest of silk between her thighs to reveal a place even she had never touched before. When he tongued her lavishly and then took her into his mouth in one greedy suckle, she cried out in lusty, wordless welcome.

Hands splayed over her bare buttocks, Landry held her firmly, burrowed deeper, drew on her still more eagerly. She was not even trying to be quiet — it would have been a hopeless effort — and he certainly did nothing to silence her cries of steadily mounting pleasure.

Finally, finally, a fierce tremor shook her, beginning in the very core of her and spreading arms of fire in every direction. "Landry," she sobbed, her hands buried in his hair, "Landry, *Landry* —"

He eased her onto the bed with the most infinite tenderness, and rose slowly, carefully, to his feet. He was breathing hard and his gaze left a path of heat as it swept over her, once and then again, hungrily. She held her arms out to him.

He was out of his trousers and shut of his boots in a moment's time. He stretched out over her, magnificent, as hard and heavy as fallen timber, even though he was holding himself in such a way as to keep from putting all his weight on her.

Her own musky scent was on his mouth when he kissed her, and started everything all over again, from the beginning, drawing all the strings inside her up tight enough to snap again, like they'd just done. Maybe harder.

The thought of that took her breath away. She'd barely survived the last round; another climb like that, to burst against the inner sky like a Chinese rocket, might just be the end of her.

Even knowing that, she wanted him, and raised her hips in an instinctive invitation. Only then did he enter her, carefully at first, and then with a powerful thrust that sent her scrambling up one side of the sky again, and the faster he moved upon her, inside her, the higher she soared.

The silent explosion happened in a place where there was no air, no clouds or stars, either. Indeed, there was nothing to see or hear, but only to feel. She clung to Landry, lest she fall forever, and felt his cries of satisfaction as he joined her there, at the edge of heaven, just seconds after her own ascent.

When it was over, they slept, arms and legs tangled, utterly spent. When Miranda opened her eyes, it was dark, and Landry was teasing one of her bare nipples into a shape he favored.

Choteau was not a large place, but it had a dress shop, a general store, and other such attractions. It might have been London or Paris, so spectacular did it appear to Miranda, who had been raised without so much as coming within looking distance of luxury. She delighted in the colorful bolts of fabric on display in the mercantile, the ready-made yarn, the barrels and crates filled with wonderful things. The smells — leather and coffee beans, books and cheese, soap and smoke from the potbellied woodstove at the heart of the store — would live in her memory forever, and always bring her honeymoon trip to Choteau to mind.

They made a number of purchases — Landry did not seem overly concerned by the costs, though Miranda thought five cents was a perfectly ridiculous price to pay for a twenty-pound sack of flour — including small gifts for the boys and a bolt of flannel to make diapers for Isaiah. Too, Landry bought several things in secret, and arranged to have them sent to Springwater by stage, refusing to tell what they were no matter how Miranda plagued him. He said she'd find out at Christmas.

Every morning, every afternoon, and every night, they made love, sometimes urgently, sometimes in long and drawn-out rounds, sometimes standing up, sometimes lying down.

"I never felt like this before," Miranda confided, on their third and last night in Choteau, snuggled next to Landry in their hotel bed, loose-limbed and sated with love-making. "All the pitching and hollering, I mean. Are we supposed to carry on like we do?"

Landry chuckled against her temple, amid the damp tendrils. He liked to let her hair down himself; it was a sure sign that he intended to make love to her, and right away. "Oh, yes," he said. "The more carrying on, the better." He kissed the side of her forehead. "I love you, Miranda," he sighed. "I never realized how lonely I was, until you came to live at my place. I thought I'd lose my mind, with you lying just down the hall, on that lumpy spare-room bed."

Miranda was as content as any mortal being had the right to be. She knew she and Landry would see their share of trouble and heartache in the years ahead, just like everybody else did over the course of a long marriage, but there would be joy, too. Laughter and mischief, plans and babies. The future stretched before her, bright as the land beyond the River Jordan, and, she sighed. "I would have taken you in," she admitted. "If you'd wanted me, I mean."

"I wanted you, Miranda," he reminded her.

"And I wanted you."

She heard a puzzled frown in his voice; it was odd, how often she heard or sensed Landry's expressions and even his thoughts. Even if she went blind the next minute, she knew she'd always be able to see him clearly in her mind's eye. "Then why didn't you let me know?"

Miranda hesitated, then took the plunge. She couldn't be holding things back from Landry if she expected their alliance to be a sound one. "I was afraid you'd think I was a loose woman. You know, since I'd had little Isaiah outside of wedlock and all."

He rolled onto his side to look into her face. "He's part of you, Isaiah is. What you did is part of you. And I *love* you, Miranda. Not just the pretty parts, like your eyes and your smile and your hair. Not just the places I like to kiss, either." She could feel his erection growing against her thigh, but most of her attention was fixed on what he was saying, on what no one had ever said to her before. "I love all the things that go together to make you who you are, good, bad, and indifferent," he finished.

She couldn't hold back the tears then. She blinked rapidly, and tried to wriggle away, in a fruitless effort to hide the fact that she was crying, but finally gave up when he wouldn't let her go, and slid her arms around his neck. "There isn't another man like you in all creation, Landry Kildare," she vowed.

"Not for you, there isn't." He grinned, showing those white teeth that she hoped her babies would have, and slid one hand down her belly to ply her shamelessly into almost instant arousal.

The sound of gunfire didn't distract them.

The sky was dark with the promise of snow, that last morning, when Landry came back to the hotel from the marshal's office down the street. Miranda was waiting in the lobby, dressed to travel and surrounded with boxes and crates containing all the wonderful things they'd bought. His expression was serious enough to worry Miranda a little.

"What is it?"

He spoke quietly, taking her arm, nodding to the boys who'd come to load their baggage into the pouchlike compartment at the rear of the stagecoach. "Some of Mike Houghton's friends tried to get him out of jail last night. The marshal and his deputies were ready for them, and Houghton was killed in the fight, along with several of the others."

Miranda felt no particular grief for Houghton's violent death — it had probably been inevitable, the way he lived — but she was sorry for the loss of a life that might have been spent in so many better ways. Experience had taught her that people didn't go bad without reason; they went wrong someplace along the way, early on usually, and just never managed to get back on the right path again. She didn't express any of her thoughts aloud, but simply nodded.

Outside, the wind was brisk, and the team of eight horses hitched to the stagecoach seemed restless, eager to run, even with a heavy burden behind them. Guffy came forward, inclined his head to Landry, took off his hat and pressed it to his chest when he turned to Miranda.

"Good to see you, Mrs. Kildare. The womenfolk up at Springwater are missing you somethin' ferocious, I hear tell." His voice took on a teasing note. "They mean to put together a quilt for you. You'll be lucky if Mrs. Doc gives back that baby, though. She's taken to him real powerful."

Miranda was eager to see and hold Isaiah, never having been away from him before. "Savannah will have a family of her own in no time," she said, and then blushed, because that was a mighty personal thing to say about a person, and to a man in the bargain.

Beside her, Landry laughed and took her elbow. "Time to board the stage for home," he said, and opened the door. He turned to Guffy, once Miranda was seated. "Any other passengers on this run?"

Guffy's voice was loud enough to echo off the mountains and roll back over them all in a wave. "No, sir. You and the missus have the coach to yourselves, all the way to Springwater."

Landry looked through the window of the coach at Miranda, wriggled his eyebrows mischievously, and grinned. "Hear that, Mrs. Kildare?" he teased. "We're traveling alone." He put just the slightest emphasis on the last word.

Miranda felt a delicious shiver move through her, and she blushed, too, but she said nothing as he climbed in and took a seat beside her, laying a proprietary hand on her knee.

The stagecoach bolted forward at a shout from Guffy, and Miranda might have tumbled to the floor if Landry hadn't caught her in the curve of his arm. Easily, he pulled her up onto his lap. By the time they were out of town, he'd arranged her astraddle of his thighs and was slowly unfastening the buttons of her dress.

"I'm going to make love to you, Mrs. Kildare," he said, matter-of-factly. "Right here, right now."

Mrs. Kildare offered no protest at all.

The employees of Thorndike Press hope you have enjoyed this Large Print book. All our Large Print titles are designed for easy reading, and all our books are made to last. Other Thorndike Press Large Print books are available at your library, through selected bookstores, or directly from us.

For information about titles, please call:

(800) 257-5157

To share your comments, please write:

Publisher
Thorndike Press
P.O. Box 159
Thorndike, Maine 04986